SHAY HEALY

*An explosive first novel from
songwriter and NIGHTHAWKS host.
Intrigue, affairs, scheming, and
wheeling and dealing – this is the
stuff of THE STUNT.*

To Ferdia McAnna
who wouldn't let me stop

THE STUNT

Shay Healy

THE O'BRIEN PRESS
DUBLIN

First published 1992 by The O'Brien Press Ltd.
20 Victoria Road, Dublin 6, Ireland

10 9 8 7 6 5 4 3 2 1

British Library Cataloguing in Publication Data
Healy, Shay
Stunt
I. Title
823 [F]

ISBN 0-86278-322-4

Cover design: David Rooney
Colour separations: City Office, Dublin
Printing: Cox & Wyman, Reading, England

One

The battered Citroen Dyane clattered into the car park of the Golden Strand Hotel. As soon as he saw the shabby white-washed walls and the broken neon sign, Danny Toner knew it was going to be another bad gig.

Danny hit the brakes and the car skidded to a halt on the gravelly surface.

'Jaysus,' Sean Devlin exclaimed from the passenger seat as he rubbed his eyes awake. 'I was having a great little fantasy. We were No. 1 in the charts, we were on the radio all day and our picture was in every newspaper and magazine in the country.'

Danny looked across at him and laughed. 'There's nothing like a long drive and a bit of dope for making superstars out of two eejits.'

The smile on Sean's face changed to an ugly scowl as he became aware of the hotel. He clasped his head and shouted angrily at Danny.

'It's a kip. A complete and utter kip. I mean, how could anybody in their right mind build such a shithouse in the middle of such beautiful countryside?'

Danny gripped the wheel and stared straight ahead. He knew Sean was speaking the truth. The Golden Strand Hotel was one of the ugliest buildings he had ever seen.

'Well? Are you going to answer me?' Sean said, punching Danny on the shoulder.

'I'm sure it looks great at night,' Danny said, trying to raise a smile from Sean.

'This is no gag, Danny,' Sean said bitterly. 'One hundred and fifty miles of slow torture to reach a bloody abattoir that sells drink.'

'Well, we might as well get out and have a peek,' Danny

said, without looking at Sean.

The two men climbed from the car and stared grim-faced at the hotel. Even the darkness of the evening could not camouflage the shoddiness of the workmanship.

'For fuck's sake, Danny,' Sean spat, 'have a look at it. I mean when are you going to learn. This is a registered morgue, with two poxy extensions that look like they've been stuck on with superglue.'

Danny looked across at Sean. 'You're a terrible pessimist, Devlin. It might be a lovely place inside.'

'How did you get talked into doing this gig?'

Danny hoped his eyes didn't give him away. He hadn't been talked into the gig by anyone. He had approached the owner himself, by telephone. He had got the number from a booking agent friend of his.

'It's not the greatest,' the agent had warned him.

'It's bread, isn't it?' Danny had countered.

When it came to selling himself, Danny was a glib salesman. The owner had not sounded very enthusiastic when Danny had told him that he was a solo performer, so quick as a flash, Danny assured him that he had a congas player as well.

'We're the smallest Caribbean band in the world.'

'And what kind of music is Caribbean music?'

'Oh y'know,' Danny said, 'a few calypsos, a bit of rock 'n' roll, a few pop tunes and a couple of Irish ballads.'

*   *   *

Sean approached the front of the building and stood at a window, under a sign which said 'Lounge'. He pointed to the poster in the window. It was a picture of Danny clutching his guitar. 'DEADLY DANNY TONER' read the legend. At the bottom there was a white space. Someone with a very shaky hand had made a spectacularly dismal effort at writing in the date.

'If you saw that poster,' Sean asked, 'would you consider that you were about to be entertained by a class act?'

''Course I would,' Danny laughed. 'That's a fine handsome fella if ever I saw one.'

'Well if you're such a wonderful guy, why did they get nineteen drunken flies to crawl into a bottle of ink and write the bit on the bottom?'

'You're just jealous,' Danny said.

'Jealous me arse! This is the fourth bucket of blood I've been suckered into by you in the past two months.'

'Suckered into?' Danny guffawed. 'Go 'way out of that, you were dyin' to do them all.'

'That's only because I kept thinking they were going to be different,' Sean said.

'And I keep tellin' you, you'll have to stop thinking in this business or else you're never going to survive.'

Sean finally relented and let a smile crease his face.

'You're a bollocks, Danny,' he laughed.

'All us artists are. Let's go on turf patrol.'

'I'm your man,' Sean said. 'Where's the pipe?'

'It's on the dashboard of the car.'

'You get the pipe and I'll get the turf,' Danny said.

Sean opened the door of the car and reached in. He took a small brass pipe from the dashboard of the car. Simultaneously, Danny rummaged in the pockets of his tight jeans, till he found the matchbox he was looking for. He opened the box and took out a small lump of greenish black hashish.

'Nice bit of black,' Danny said, his eyes lighting up. 'Better than that crap we smoked on the way down.'

'Don't you go criticising my dope,' Sean said in mock huffed tones.

'Fill that fucker up,' Danny said, passing Sean the lump of dope.

'It's nice and moist,' Sean said, feeling the texture of the hashish. 'There must be a moxy of oil in it. I hope it lifts my head off.'

'We'd better sit into the car,' Danny said. 'No point in getting off to a bad start with the proprietors of this place.'

They climbed into the car. Sean lit the pipe, inhaled and blew the smoke across at Danny and passed him the pipe at the same time. Danny inhaled deeply. The first mouthful caught at the back of his throat, almost making him cough. 'That's quare oul' turf all the same,' he spluttered, as he passed the pipe back to Sean.

'It'd want to be,' Sean said. 'I've a feeling we're going to need a major anaesthetic tonight.'

'D'you want to go inside and see what the story is?'

The two men finished smoking, climbed from the car and started walking towards the front door of the hotel.

'I'm very stoned,' Danny said, making two attempts at pulling the door open. Sean reached across him and pushed the door gently inwards.

'After you, Dumbo,' he laughed.

'No. After you,' Danny insisted.

'Try the bar there,' Sean said.

Danny pushed open the door marked 'Bar'. The bar was small, about fourteen feet by sixteen. It had an assortment of unmatched tables and cheap stools, with a long bench seat running along the partition wall facing the door.

Two men were standing at either end of the counter, separated by several high stools and a heavy silence. They looked like farmers. One wore a battered cap and a heavy tweed jacket, although the day had been sunny and warm. The other man wore a cheap nylon shirt with the sleeves rolled up unevenly. Braces and a wide leather belt held up a pair of grey pants that hung listlessly from a huge belly.

'Dig the crap-catcher pants,' Danny muttered. 'Is there

anybody about?' he asked loudly.

'He's out the back there somewhere,' the one with the cap said, pointing with his glass through the archway that led from the bar into the lounge.

'Thanks,' Danny said. He turned and bumped into Sean.

They paused outside the door marked 'Lounge'.

'What d'ya bet there won't be six beautiful chicks inside here having the crack, getting all bevvied up for a barbecue outside their caravan tonight?' Danny laughed.

'You're a terrible dreamer,' Sean grimaced.

Danny pushed open the door. Sean stuck his head over Danny's shoulder and had a quick look around.

'Mother of Jaysus,' Sean said, 'this kip gets worse and fucking worse.'

The lounge had the same graceless formica charm as the rest of the hotel. In behind the counter, a man of about forty-five was bent over the bar, reading the racing page of the *Irish Press*. His head was large and pear-shaped and on top of it was a really ill-fitting toupee, sitting at a slight angle to the rest of the hair. The difference in colour between the toupee and the natural hair made it look even more preposterous. He had small, piggy, pink eyes, a bulbous nose and thin lips that clung together in the kind of thin, corrugated line that cartoonists use to convey drunkenness.

'Did you cop the state of the toupee?' Danny spluttered quietly over his shoulder. 'It looks like it made a forced landing.'

Sean stifled a guffaw.

'How's it going?' Danny breezed, as he and Sean approached the counter. 'Brilliant day, wasn't it?' Danny continued, not giving the bartender a chance to talk until he had completed his opening spiel. 'I'm Danny Toner and this is my drummer, Sean Devlin. We're here for the gig tonight.'

The toupee shifted slightly as the bartender raised his

head. He paused for what seemed like an eternity. 'Right,' he grunted, the corner of the corrugated mouth opening like a clam taking a peek for passing enemies.

'We're wondering where we should set up the gear,' Danny prattled on, undaunted by the hostile grunts.

'Ye won't be too loud, will ye?'

'Not at all,' Danny answered, still smiling away cheerfully. 'It's only a one-hundred-watt PA, so it'll be nice and quiet. Sure you'll hardly hear us when the place is full. Does it fill up on a Tuesday?'

'Sometimes it does and sometimes it doesn't.'

Sean marvelled at the way Danny kept to his task, chatting away as though he were making small talk with an old friend.

'Well, do you think we should set up there in the corner near the window, or should we move the pool table and work from there?'

'I don't know,' came the gruff answer. 'It was me brother who booked ye and he's not here at the minute.'

'Fair enough,' Danny said. 'Tell us, would you know what room we're staying in? Maybe we could freshen up and then get a bit of grub, before we set up the gear.'

'Right,' came the grunt again. 'Hold on and I'll get ye a key, but ye won't get any grub yet. The chef is away off for a swim and the kitchen doesn't open till seven tonight.'

Danny turned and looked at Sean as the pear-shaped head disappeared through a door at the back of the bar. 'Now there's a bundle of laughs,' Danny said.

'And I'll bet you the Grunting Toupee will be the same man we'll have to get the readies from at the end of the night,' Sean said.

'Right,' Danny said, doing a wickedly accurate impersonation of the bartender.

'I'll tell you somethin', Danny,' Sean said, 'I want you always to treat me well. I'm a very rare friend that has soldiered with you through these buckets of blood. This is an unmitigated kip and I'm an eejit for being here.'

'Sure we'll have a few fucking laughs,' Danny smiled.

Sean didn't have time to answer. The bartender was coming through the door carrying a key.

'Here ye are. Ye're in No. 10.'

'Fair enough,' Danny said. 'Will your brother be back shortly?'

'He might and he mightn't.'

'Well, when he does come back, would you ask him to give us a shout in the room please?'

'Right.'

Two

As he crossed from O'Connell Bridge to Westmoreland Street, Stephen 'Snake' O'Reilly edged a few feet to his right so he could catch a glimpse of his reflection in the window of the News and Leisure shop on the corner.

He was pleased with what he saw. He was wearing a dapper grey suit with a short boxed jacket. The pants flared slightly from the waist, tapering again at the ankle. A crisp white shirt, a thin black leather tie with a tiny knot and a pair of pointed slip-on leather shoes gave him a hard, clean image, which emphasised his strong angular features, his thin lips and his cold eyes.

The silver metal briefcase rounded off the overall sharpness. He was really pleased with the briefcase. To Snake, the metal briefcase epitomised success as a rock band manager. It was the ultimate accessory.

Snake's mind was on fire. He had just called to see his friend and fellow band manager, Tony Doyle, who had flipped out over the tape and the photographs of Poison Pig. 'I swear, it's brilliant.'

'You wouldn't spoof me?' Snake had asked defensively.

'You know me, I say what I think.'

Now Snake was on his way to meet a journalist from *Hot Press*. He was hoping the magazine would agree to do a full-page interview with Poison Pig.

Poison Pig had been conceived after a night in a club on Leeson Street. Snake had been snorting coke all evening in the company of rival managers and as usual the conversation had turned to music.

'I've got a pain in me dick with them all,' Snake said. 'There isn't an original band in the whole town.'

'That's a bit of an exaggeration,' someone said.

'Oh is it?' Snake snapped. 'Well, walk by Temple Lane Studios, or any of those other rehearsal studios and all you can hear are bad imitations of U2. Sometimes I think it was a fuck-up that U2 became so big. All we have now are a load of U2s and a load of guys wanting to be the Messiah, like Bono.'

'Yeah, it's crazy, isn't it?' said someone else.

'I'm not knockin' Bono or Geldof or Sting or any of those other blokes, but all this saving people is gettin' out of hand. I think it's absolutely pathetic,' Snake said. 'You've got Sting and Springsteen and a million rock stars all wired-up and now, because of the likes of Geldof and Bono, the whole bloody world wants to go up on the cross.'

'That's what the world seems to want at the moment,' someone else said.

'Wouldn't it be great if there was a band which said "Fuck the world – let's get on with the music." I bet it would work,' Snake laughed.

'Yeah and cost a fortune.'

Snake didn't flinch at the mention of money. Unlike his band manager friends who relied on their bands for their income, Snake was pulling in six hundred pounds a week from three discos he ran in tennis and rugby clubs in the south city. His career as an entrepreneur had begun when he charged family and friends one pound each to attend his fourteenth birthday party, at which he had also acted as DJ. His profit amounted to thirty-four pounds and a hustler was born.

By the time he was eighteen, Snake had started his first teenage disco in a rugby club, and once he had learnt how to recruit and deal with bouncers his natural skills as a promoter had begun to flourish. His gigs were trouble-free, so parents were happy to let their teenagers attend, and as soon as he had got the taste of money he had bought himself a Golf GTi and begun insinuating himself into the rock-music fraternity.

Snake loved every minute of his new existence. He hung out in the Pink Elephant and the Bailey and learned to speak the argot of rock 'n' roll. He kept his ears and eyes open all the time and wasn't shy when it came to asking questions about record contracts and publishing deals. He wangled his way backstage at all the major rock gigs and his name cropped up regularly in the gossip columns of magazines and newspapers. It was no surprise when he announced he was to manage a band called Honeysuckle.

Honeysuckle was a mess from the moment Snake became involved. He fell madly in love with Rose Meany, the lead singer, who was a better dancer than she was a singer. Blinded by love, Snake spent all of his savings making demos and flying record company executives to Dublin to see the band. His enthusiasm and ardour became a trial for everyone around him and it wasn't until he found himself two thousand pounds in debt to the bank that Snake realised that being a band manager wasn't as easy as it looked and being in love was destructive to the ambitions of a young tycoon like himself.

With characteristic single-mindedness, Snake dropped the band and ended his relationship with Rose Meany. He concentrated on his teenage discos and expanded his business by buying an eight-track recording studio. He kept it permanently busy by offering good deals to struggling bands. As soon as he had paid off his overdraft and money had begun to flow again, Snake swore to himself that he would never get involved with another band until he was sure he could make it work as a business.

Now, at twenty-six, Snake was ready to become a manager again. He had sold the recording studio, and with his steady income of six hundred pounds a week he had no trouble getting an overdraft from the bank.

When he woke after his night out, Snake's brain was still racing. The idea of a band who would scoff at all the do-gooders in rock really appealed to him and with his usual fervour he set about making it a reality. The four members of Poison Pig were chosen carefully after long hours of information-gathering and observation. He could have found a band that was already established as a unit and worked at giving them an image, but the more he thought about it, the more he realised that the members of the band would have to have a complete awareness of what they were doing.

Snake looked at a lot of singers before he finally decided on Danny Toner as his lead singer. Danny had natural charisma and charm. He stood six feet two, with broad shoulders tapering to a slim waist and muscular hips. Warm, penetrating blue eyes, a strong nose, full sensuous lips and a fine mane of black hair gave Danny a raffish air. When he applied stage make-up, the image became more sinister. Black eye-liner made him look slightly depraved. Artificial dark shadows under his cheekbones gave him a high-fashion anorexic face and the hint of red lipstick turned his mouth into a provocative pout.

Danny's clothes were thrift-shop chic, tuxedo jackets, fringed leather jackets, even striped boating blazers. Around his neck, he wore a gold devil's head, with ruby eyes. Snake had had it for years and at last he had found some real use for it. Danny also wore a small jet earring in his left ear and from his buttonhole he hung a small wooden coffin, about two inches along, bearing a brass plate with the inscription 'RIP – The World.'

*   *   *

When Snake first approached him, Danny was playing in a band in Slattery's Bar in Capel Street. Some nights they got five pounds a man and some nights they got fifteen. Before that he had been through a succession of bands, sometimes playing keyboards, sometimes guitar. Danny was a good musician and a confident singer. He was also known for his natural rapport with an audience. At nineteen he had married his childhood sweetheart, Mary Tiernan, because she was pregnant. Now at twenty-four he was the father of two children, Deirdre and Danny Junior. The economics of survival had been getting very serious when Snake approached him. Danny listened to what Snake had to say.

'Will I get a wage while the band is rehearsing?'

'I think I can arrange that,' Snake replied.

'What about clothes and stuff?'

'I'll give you an allowance for clothes as well.'

'OK, I'm in,' Danny said.

Once Danny was in the band, Snake knew he would have little trouble recruiting Sean Devlin on drums. He and Danny were best friends, but Sean also had a very solid reputation both as an amicable character and as a drummer. He was content to remain in the background and let Danny do most of the talking, but when push came to shove, he was well able to state his opinion and his solid build and strong chiselled face made him look bigger than his five foot ten inches.

'I'd like to talk to Danny first, before I make a decision,' Sean told Snake.

Next, Snake courted Frankie Dunn as lead guitarist. Frankie was a pushover for Snake, who merely had to paint a picture of limousines, VIP lounges and pretty girls to get his full attention. Best of all, Frankie was totally malleable in terms of dress and behaviour in the band. Already he looked the part in his black leather jacket and black leather pants, and once Snake explained what the band was about, he knew Frankie would be no trouble.

'Fuck the world – I'm into saving rock 'n' roll.' Frankie smiled as he repeated Snake's words aloud. 'Yeah, I can dig that.'

Choosing Richie Killen to play bass caused Snake the most anxiety. Richie was a recovering heroin addict, who had suffered a couple of relapses before a protracted stay in the Coolmine Drug Treatment Centre had finally got him clean. Snake took a lot of counsel from musicians and managers before he finally decided to take a chance on Richie.

When Snake saw all four together for the first time he knew that Richie's little-boy-lost appeal was a perfect complement to Danny's exuberance, Sean's solidity and Frankie's showiness. Richie's small, thin body cried out for a hug and the bass looked almost too heavy in his hands.

'The women go mad for you, I hear,' Snake said to Richie.

'I don't know about that,' Richie answered, smiling shyly. 'They never seem to stick around very long.'

*　　*　　*

The International Bar was cool and uncrowded. Snake sat back into the comfortable leather seat and sipped at his pint of lemonade shandy. The journalist had sent a message saying he would be a few minutes late and Snake was using the time to compose his thoughts.

He lifted the metal briefcase on to the table in front of him and opened it, snapping the metal locks loud enough to cause the other drinkers to look around. Snake took a photograph and a cassette from the case, closed it and replaced it on the floor. He looked at the photograph of Poison Pig. It looked superb.

The balance is perfect, Snake thought. Danny dominated the line-up. Beside him Sean Devlin looked solidly angry, his hint of stubble adding to his toughness. Richie Killen, with sad dark eyes and a soft face, clutched his bass guitar as though it was a lifeline someone had thrown him. Frankie Dunn, the lead guitarist, leered out of the photograph. He was the only one who bore anything resembling a smile, but it had a jeering quality about it that made Snake chuckle.

The inlay card for the cassette was a variation of the photograph. It had the band's name, Poison Pig, and the titles of four songs printed on it.

'Hello there. Sorry I'm late.'

Snake looked up to see the tall bespectacled figure of the journalist standing over him.

'What'll you have?' Snake asked.

'A nice cold pint of lager would go down well.'

'No problem. Here, there's a photograph of the band, while I'm getting you your drink.'

Three

Jeannie Callanan heard the click of the back door closing. She rose from where she had been sitting on the bed and moved quickly to the window. Below her she saw her mother come around the corner of the house, walk down the short path and out the front gate.

Her mother stopped at the front gate, turned and threw a glance up at Jeannie's window. Jeannie jumped back behind the curtain. She held her breath for an instant and then she took another quick peep to make sure she knew which direction her mother had taken. Jeannie's mother turned right and Jeannie breathed a sigh of relief, knowing that she was heading up the winding road that climbed the hill behind the house.

The modern three-bedroomed bungalow was so quiet now that Jeannie could hear the clock ticking. Outside, the warm sun was still shining brightly. All day Jeannie had stayed locked in her room, refusing to talk to either her mother or her father. Now that she was alone in the house, she felt a little more relaxed, but she knew she would have to move fast.

Jeannie picked up a photograph from her dressing-table. She was smiling in the photograph, standing between her mother and her father. She was twelve years old when the picture had been taken, back in her happy days when she lived in Dublin. Why the family had ever left the capital had been a mystery to Jeannie. She remembered what a lively person her mother had been when they had lived there, always rushing off on the bus, coming home laden with little gifts for Jeannie.

When she was twelve, Jeannie had asked her parents for the millionth time why she did not have a brother or sister. Her mother had sat her down in the kitchen across the table from her, never taking her eyes from Jeannie's eyes.

'A year after you were born,' she began, 'I was expecting another baby, but it wasn't in the right place, so they had to open me up. And when they did, they found something growing in my womb, which is where I should have been carrying my baby, so they had to take away my womb.'

'Did they have to take the baby away too?'

'Yes, they did,' her mother answered, her eyes moistening at the memory.

'And were you very upset?'

'Yes.'

'Was Daddy sad as well?'

'Yes, Daddy was very sad.'

This was one of the few clues Jeannie had to her father's intimate feelings. He was a closed, quiet man, not given to communicating. His wife and daughter simply went along with it when he proposed moving to the country. Perhaps it was his need to isolate himself that drove him away.

For the first year, after they had moved to the fifteen-acre farm on an exposed hillside in the far south-west of Ireland, everyone in the family had worked hard, including Jeannie, who had taken on the job of looking after the twenty-five hens who lived in a small hen-run at the back of the house. It had been hard getting used to the quiet. Even though as a family they had lived quietly in Dublin, Jeannie and her mother missed the comforting bustle of the city. Not having close neighbours had also been a strain. It had thrown the three of them together constantly. Most nights they sat silently watching television until it was time for bed.

'Do you like it here?' her mother asked one night, when Jeannie's father was still out in the fields.

'It's all right,' Jeannie answered.

'Tell me the truth,' her mother asked softly.

'I hate it,' Jeannie blurted out, tears springing to her eyes.

'I know, I know,' her mother said, and she seemed to be agreeing with her daughter.

*　　*　　*

Jeannie looked at her full-length reflection in the mirror. Only the surprising fullness of her breasts gave any clue to her age. Tomorrow she would be eighteen. Tomorrow she would be free, gone from this house that she hated so much. The note to her mother, which was propped against the jewellery box on her dressing-table, had taken Jeannie hours to write. She had tried to find an easy way to say goodbye, but she knew that no matter how she said it, her mother would be crushed. She said she would keep in contact and send them a phone number but asked them not to come after her to get her to come back. She really wanted to try things on her own for a while.

As she picked up her rucksack, tears welled up in her eyes. She took a last lingering look around and then she ran from the room. She ran down the stairs, out through the front door, running down the path, out through the gate, the tears blinding her eyes. She turned and started running down the hill, afraid to look over her shoulder in case her courage might fail her.

When she reached the bottom of the hill, Jeannie dabbed at her eyes with a tissue, trying not to smudge the eye make-up she had so carefully applied. Anxiously, she looked at her watch. She would take a lift going either direction. She prayed her father's car would not appear around the corner. Ten minutes passed without any traffic. Then a yellow van appeared around the bend in the road. Jeannie shyly stuck her thumb up. The van slowed to a halt. A genial middle-aged man was driving.

'I'm only going a few miles out, as far as the Golden Strand Hotel, if that's any good to you,' he said.

'That would be fine,' Jeannie said, as she climbed into the passenger seat.

Jeannie slumped down in her seat as they drove, frightened that her father might see her. She let her thoughts freewheel. Hypnotised by the hedgerows speeding past the windows of the van, she drifted into a silent half-sleep.

'We're here.' The driver's voice brought her out of her trance. She thanked him, climbed from the van and walked through the gateway of the Golden Strand Hotel.

Two young men were lifting microphones and speakers from the back of a Citroen Dyane. One was tall and handsome, with a mane of black hair. His jeans and T-shirt clung to a lean, muscular body. The second man was shorter and stockier. He also wore blue jeans and a bright Hawaiian shirt. The taller man caught sight of Jeannie as she shyly approached the hotel. Without taking his eyes off her, he reached out and poked the other man with his finger. The second man turned and looked.

'I told you there'd be a few crackers,' laughed the first man, his laughter tinkling on the warm evening breeze.

Jeannie felt her face redden and then the tall handsome man gave her a big friendly wink.

'Hiya,' Danny said.

'Hello,' Jeannie answered shyly.

'I hope you're coming for our gig tonight?'

'Are you in a band?' Jeannie asked shyly.

'My good woman, you are looking at the smallest Caribbean band in the world,' chortled Danny. 'I'm Danny and this is Sean,' he continued. 'What's your name?'

'Jeannie Callanan,' she told him.

'Are you coming to stay here?'

She was flustered by his question. 'I'm not sure,' she replied. 'I'm hoping I might get a lift to Dublin tonight.'

'Tonight!' Danny said. 'That's a pity. We're not going back until the morning.'

'We don't have any room either,' interjected Sean in a whisper, behind Danny's back.

Danny looked hard at Jeannie. 'We have to get this sound

21

gear set up, but when we're finished we'll be having a drink in the lounge, so if you want to join us, please feel free.'

'Thanks,' Jeannie said. 'I might do that.' She smiled, trying to look like she was in complete command. 'I think I'll just sit out here on the window ledge and catch the last bit of sun.'

Jeannie watched as they carried the sound equipment into the lounge. She had fifty-five pounds in her purse and she knew she would have to watch every penny of it carefully.

'Ooh, I'm in love,' Danny laughed, as he plugged in the microphone to the amplifier.

'Jaysus, so am I,' Sean said. 'She's a little darling.'

'Seems like a nice kid too,' Danny said. 'What age d'you think she is?'

'About twelve,' Sean laughed.

'You're just trying to put me off because you want her for yourself.'

'Well, you know us single men,' Sean said airily. 'We have to be constantly on the look-out for a suitable partner.'

'Go 'way, you dirty bastard,' Danny laughed. 'As if you being single would make any difference. Sure you'd ride Superman's mother – and she's a married woman.'

Danny fiddled with the knobs on the amplifier. 'Go out there and see how it sounds.'

'Would it not be better if I heard how it sounds?' Sean asked sarcastically.

'Jaysus, YOU'RE A DESPERATE SMART-ASS.' Danny's words boomed through the microphone.

'That sounds grand,' Sean called from the back of the room. 'Now try the other one.'

'ONE TWO, ONE TWO, ONE TWO.'

'I hear you're going back to college,' Sean shouted.

'What for?' Danny asked.

'To learn to count up to three so that you can become a professional microphone tester,' Sean laughed.

'C'mon, asshole,' Danny said, flicking off the power switch on the amplifier. 'Let's get a drink.'

Danny walked to the window, where he could see Jeannie sitting on the ledge with her back to him. He knocked at the window and mimed drinking from a glass. Jeannie looked at him and nodded a smiling Yes.

* * *

Danny rose. 'I'll go and see if there's any chance of a bit of food.' Jeannie and Sean sat in awkward silence.

'Danny's a really nice guy, isn't he?' Jeannie said, finally breaking the silence.

Sean looked at her. He could see from her expression that Danny had worked his charm one more time. Sean knew Danny's routine well. Danny had been attentive, asking questions, letting Jeannie do most of the talking.

'He's a nice guy if you like a smart-ass gorilla,' Sean said.

'Do you two ever stop slagging each other?'

'Not if we can help it.'

Danny came walking back through the door. 'Dinner is served in the dining-room presently. I ordered chicken, chips and peas for the three of us. It looked like the safest thing on the menu.'

'Did you order for me?' Jeannie asked.

''Course I did,' Danny laughed. 'I told him you were our publicist.'

Jeannie was glad of Danny's kindness. She hadn't eaten all day and the hot hunger pains had not been eased by the two glasses of shandy she had drunk.

As they sipped coffee after the meal, Sean looked across the table at Danny. 'Turf patrol?'

'Great idea,' Danny agreed. 'We also have to do a list of songs.'

Jeannie moved shyly to get up from the table.

'Well, I'd better be off, especially if you're busy.'

The helpless tone in her voice touched Danny.

'Hold on a minute. Nobody's getting rid of you. What are you going to do?'

'I'll walk back up to the main road,' Jeannie said, 'and see if I can get a lift to Dublin.'

'Sure at this stage it'll be all hours by the time you get to Dublin,' Danny said. 'Have you somewhere to stay there?'

'I have an aunt,' Jeannie lied, reaching for her rucksack.

'Wait a second, wait a second,' Danny put his hand on her arm. He turned to Sean. 'Hey, Magoo, is there any chance if we repacked the gear that we could fit herself here into the Dyane?'

Sean looked from Danny to Jeannie. She looked like a helpless puppy.

'I suppose we could,' Sean grinned. 'There's not much of her in it anyway.'

'What'll happen if you don't get there tonight?' Danny asked.

'It wouldn't really matter,' Jeannie said hesitantly. 'I didn't say that I was coming today for definite.'

'That's it so,' Danny said. 'You can stay here the night with us. Myself and Sean have a room here in the hotel. There are only two beds, but we can stick them together and sleep across them, if you don't mind a bit of discomfort.'

A shadow of apprehension scuttled across Jeannie's eyes.

'You needn't worry,' Danny assured her. 'Myself and dick-brain here are totally harmless and we won't touch you. Sure we won't, Sean.'

'Safe as a house –' Sean laughed, '– on fire.'

Jeannie looked from one to the other. Both of them were smiling at her.

'OK,' Jeannie said. 'If it's all right with you.'

The shaft of sunlight that first knifed its way through the curtained window of Richie Killen's flat shone like a spotlight on a photograph of Richie and his mother. The arc of light travelled slowly, picking out different highlights as it moved. For a long time it illuminated Richie's bass guitar, which leaned up against the small practice amplifier. Then it travelled along the floor, lighting his red Converse All-Star basketball boots, gliding slowly over his crumpled jeans, ascending along the sheets and across the pillow, until the heat and the light on his eyelids brought him blinkingly awake.

Richie pulled one arm in front of his eyes to shield them from the light. With the other arm, he searched blindly for the small metal alarm clock, which sat on the bedside table. His fingers closed around the metal and he pulled the clock close to his face, squinting to read the time.

The shaft of light told Richie that it was a warm day outside, but still he felt a shiver run through him.

'Dear Jesus,' Richie said softly.

A familiar panic gripped him. His chest and stomach felt tight. A strange kind of pressure made him feel like everything in his body was rushing to his head. He had the urge to jump from the bed and run, anywhere, any direction.

'Breathe,' Richie told himself. 'Breathe.'

Richie took in great big breaths, inhaling and exhaling evenly. After a few minutes, he felt the panic subsiding and he pulled back the sheet and swung his legs over the side of the bed.

If only Mam were alive, Richie thought to himself. She would calm me down. She would soothe me. He fought the urge to be sick, picking up the half joint that was still in the ashtray from the night before. He lit it and inhaled deeply, willing the dope to work fast. After a few minutes he felt the familiar buzz in his system. Richie knew he only had a few minutes to get himself together. Frankie would be calling for him soon to take him to a meeting with Snake. Richie knew that he must not let Snake or any member of the band know just how shaky he felt.

He opened the curtains and sunlight flooded the room. It had an immediate calming effect on him. He remembered what his mother used to say. 'Let the light in first, Richie, and happiness will follow.'

His mother had been at his bedside the first time Richie had woken from an overdose.

'I want to die, Mam. Why didn't they let me die?'

'No, my baby,' his mother had said, stroking his hair. 'You have so much to live for and you're going to live and get better and I'm going to take care of you.'

'Oh Mam, I let you down. I told you I'd look after myself and I didn't. I swear I'll go clean. I'll do anything you want. I promise.'

'Come home. Your bedroom is still there waiting for you.'

'I can't, Mam,' Richie said. 'I have to prove to Dad that I can make it on my own.'

'Listen, Richie, you and your father have your differences, but I know that if you decide to come home, he'll be as glad as I am.'

'Well maybe it's not Dad I have to prove something to, Mam. Maybe it's myself.'

'Will you stay off the drugs? Promise me you will.'

'I will, Mam, I will.'

It was his father who first told Richie of his mother's illness.

'I'm afraid your mother isn't very well.'

'What's wrong with her?'

'Well, you know the pain she's had in her side for such a

long time now, the doctors are a bit worried about it, so they're taking her in next week to have a look at it.'

'Is Mam going to be all right?'

'They're doing everything they can for her.'

Over the next nine months, Richie's mother died slowly and painfully. Many times after her death Richie had tried to talk to his father, but each time he had sat down to do it, the forbidding stern face had stopped him. In his own grief and loneliness, his father had become more unapproachable than ever.

Richie tried hard to keep some of his mother's love flowing towards his younger brother and sisters. He had taught himself to cook and to keep the house tidy while his mother was ill. He assumed the role of mother, trying to be there when the children arrived home from school. But no matter how hard he tried, Richie still had to put up with the complaints from his father.

'I come home from a hard day at the office and all I find is my family watching television. Nobody's doing any homework. Instead you're just lounging around wasting your time. Not paying any heed to the future. If your mother were alive today she'd be horrified. I don't know what kind of a family I reared.'

'I'll tell you what kind of a family you reared,' Richie said. 'You didn't rear any kind of a family. Mam reared us. She gave us a bit of love and she didn't expect us to be perfect all the time. All you do is shout and complain. Well, have a good look at your family. We're all going through the same pain as you over Mam, but the two girls are still children and Colin is still not exactly an adult, so what the fuck do you expect from them?'

A fist exploded into the side of Richie's head. For an instant he was stunned. He shook his head and saw his father glaring angrily at him.

'Don't you ever use that kind of language to me again, sonny boy.'

Richie hurled himself at his father. His momentum carried them both against the cabinet that stood by the sitting-room wall.

'I'll fucking kill you, you bastard,' Richie cried, his hands clawing at his father's face.

His sisters, Aileen and Veronica, began to cry. His brother Colin came running from the kitchen, throwing his arms around Richie's shoulders to stop him throwing punches at his father. Aileen, tears streaming down her face, grabbed hold of Richie's leg.

'Please, Richie, please. Please stop.'

Through his blazing anger, Richie heard the child's voice.

'All right, all right.' Richie stroked the top of Aileen's head. 'It's going to be all right.' He looked back at his father. 'If I ever hear of you hitting one of these kids, I'll beat the living daylights out of you.'

Richie whirled and walked quickly from the room, up the stairs to his bedroom. He crossed to his small dressing-table and opened the top drawer. He took out a small box and opened it. Inside was a small lump of hash. As he rolled a joint, Richie knew he could no longer stay in the same house with his father. His brother and sisters needed him, but he knew that if he stayed he would be no good to them. He needed all his strength to save himself. If he cracked up again, he knew he would have no one to save him this time.

Tears began to roll down Richie's cheeks. He turned his head and looked at the framed picture of himself and his mother, which stood on his bedside table. The two of them were smiling, Richie's arm draped affectionately around her shoulders. Richie picked up the photograph and clutching it to his chest, he fell onto the bed like a man who had been shot.

'Mam, Mam, what am I going to do?'

Five

A warm evening quiet had settled on the centre of Dublin as Snake O'Reilly hurried up Grafton Street. The city's most fashionable shopping street was almost deserted, with only the singing of a lone musician breaking the silence.

Snake was feeling mighty pleased with himself as he strode towards the Bailey. His meeting with the journalist had gone well and the interview was all set for the next morning. He had contacted Richie and Frankie and later he would ring Danny and Sean.

The Bailey was Snake's main social arena. He liked the extreme brightness of the pub. He loved to feel the envious glances of young rock musicians and aspiring band managers. Even better, he loved the admiring glances of the young girls, with their spiky haircuts, their long lace evening gloves and their outrageous dresses.

A friendly wave caught Snake's attention. His hairdresser, Billy Quinn, was calling him over to a small table in the alcove, just inside the side door.

'The very man,' Snake said. 'Any whizz, Billy?'

'How much do you want?' Billy asked.

'Just enough for a couple of lines tonight. My regular bloke is away until tomorrow. I'll be able to give it back to you tomorrow night.'

'That's cool, that's cool,' Billy said. 'Have a drink and I'll organise that for you in a minute.'

Three tequilas later, Snake looked at his watch. 'Holy shit! It's eleven o'clock. I'm gone, gang.' Snake rose from the table, touching the small packet of speed in his jacket pocket.

'See you later,' Snake said, as he pushed his way through the now crowded bar. Using his metal briefcase like an ice-breaker, he cut a passage for himself through the throng which was three deep at the bar.

Snake hurried back onto Grafton Street and cut across Johnson's Court to Clarendon Street.

Earlier in the day, Snake had parked his car on Clarendon Street, knowing that his itinerary would eventually bring him back around there in the evening. Snake's admiration for his own astute planning was rudely shattered when he saw the parking ticket under the windscreen wiper.

'Bastards,' he muttered. He slammed the car into first gear and accelerated away from the kerb.

After a quick drive, Snake stopped half-way down a terrace of narrow redbrick houses. He got out of the car and pushed the doorbell of No. 10. A light flicked on in the hallway and the door opened to reveal Mary Toner, Danny's wife.

'That's some nine o'clock,' she rebuked him in her musical south County Dublin accent.

'I was trying to get us some speed,' Snake said, reaching for her.

'Get off,' she laughed. 'Not here in the fizzin' hall.'

He followed her through the tiny sitting-room into the equally tiny kitchen. He pushed her up against the refrigerator door and kissed her hard on the mouth, pushing his tongue roughly between her teeth. She returned his kiss with the same intensity, her hand tightening on the back of his neck.

Snake was conscious of the metal briefcase still in his hand. He bent his knees to set it down. Without taking his lips from hers, he slid her down along the refrigerator door, bumping her gently onto the floor so that her flowery summer skirt rode up around her creamy sun-tanned thighs.

'Hold it, hold it,' Mary panted. 'Jesus, Snake, you arrive two hours late and now you want to treat me like a quick ride.'

'Sorry, kid. I'm sorry. I can't help myself diving at you.'

'Yeah,' Mary said sceptically, cocking an eyebrow.

'It's true,' Snake protested. 'Of all the women I have ever met, you are the horniest.' He paused. 'You're also beautiful and intelligent and sometimes I wonder how you got stuck with a dreamer like Danny.'

The words stung Mary like icy raindrops on her face. Where was the dreamer she had fallen for, the beguiling laughing Danny who had swept her up and carried her along with his mad notions and his boundless energy, his passion for life and his unselfish love. Somewhere along the way, the Danny who had shared every thought, every dream with her, had become remote, less physical, lost in his own struggle to make his mark on the world. His head was somewhere else, outside home, outside their relationship.

In the beginning, Danny had brought her everywhere, and even when young Danny was born, it had merely added another person to the mad cavalcade that always seemed to follow in Danny's wake, a caravan of madness, laughter and good times.

Mary knew that Danny hated a lot of the gigs he had to endure, but his moods were a part of him that she had come to accommodate and she knew that some gentle talk and a few warm hugs would always bring him out of his gloom. But Poison Pig had changed him, and she couldn't tell whether he was happy or not. She felt powerless to ask questions and Danny seemed reluctant to let her know anything of what was going on.

At first, Mary had thought she was imagining that Snake was coming on to her. He paid her endless compliments, and when he phoned looking for Danny he always seemed to take extra time to talk to her before speaking to Danny. Snake's dynamism was so different to Danny's. His outlook was much more materialistic, but Mary couldn't help liking the drive and energy he put into Poison Pig and into his own ventures. He was so much more pragmatic than Danny, and, in spite of herself, she couldn't help envying the wad of notes that Snake constantly carried in his pocket. She wondered what life would be like if she had money to indulge herself with new clothes, shoes, make-up and decent haircuts, all the luxuries that were missing from her life with Danny.

'I spotted these on the Portobello Road and I thought they were very *you*,' Snake had said one day, dropping a pair of crystal earrings onto the kitchen table. It was the first time he had ever done anything other than compliment her. Mary was taken aback. Danny was out with Sean and Snake had called in on his way back from the airport.

Mary picked up the crystals, set in silver and looked at them. What does he mean by 'really *me*', she wondered. Does he still see me as a middle-class south County Dublin hippy who wears long floral-print skirts and scarves in her long blond hair? Do I look like the archetypal free spirit, an alien in Snake's ordered world?

'Thank you,' Mary said, hesitantly fingering the earrings. 'They're very nice.' She leaned over to give Snake a peck of gratitude on the cheek, but suddenly they were kissing passionately, and then his hands were sliding up under her T-shirt. She gasped with excitement and then pulled away.

'Wait, Snake ... give me a minute.'

'No,' Snake said. 'I know you want me. And I want you.' Roughly he pulled her to him.

'You'll have to wear a condom,' she whispered, hoping it would not put him off.

'That's OK,' he said.

It was so different from Danny's lovemaking. Mary had never made love to anyone else and many times she had wondered how different it might be. Now Snake was licking her neck, licking her thighs and she felt a fire that was totally new to her and she responded by guiding him into her and wrapping her legs around his waist.

After the first time, she suffered enormous guilt, but as Danny's indifference towards her continued, Mary found herself responding to Snake more and more and soon he was sneaking to her whenever he knew Danny would be gone for a few hours. The novelty and the excitement were electric in the beginning, but over the weeks Mary had become more irritated at the way Snake breezed in and out, stopping only to make love before leaving with some plausible excuse about business still to be done, even though it was the early hours of the morning.

'Did Danny ring you yet, by the way?'

Snake's question snapped Mary back to attention.

'No,' she answered. 'And I don't expect him to.'

'Well, did he say before he left what time the session would finish?'

'What session?' Mary asked.

'The session he's doing in Glasthule.'

Mary threw back her head and laughed.

'There's no session! Himself and Sean are gone off doing some awful gig in Limerick or Kerry or somewhere.'

'You're not fucking serious!'

Snake was on his feet, his eyes blazing with anger.

'Yes, I am,' Mary said, the smile fading from her face.

Snake stood fuming, his words tumbling out like machine-gun fire. 'I have a full-page interview set up for eleven o'clock tomorrow morning and the silly fucker goes off to do some crappy gig in the back of beyond.'

'Don't be too hard on him,' Mary said, a hint of defensiveness creeping into her voice. 'The phone was cut off this morning and we're two months behind on the mortgage. We need the money and it's not exactly coming from gigs with the band.'

Snake heard the biting tone in Mary's voice. He let his anger subside.

'You're right, you're right,' Snake said, dragging his hand exasperatedly through his hair. 'It's just that it's taken me quite a while to set up this interview and I can't ring them now and tell them to cancel. Is Danny staying away over-night?'

'As far as I know, he is,' Mary said. 'I think it's part of the deal.'

'In that case we're fucked,' Snake said. 'I'll have to go along by myself and I'll look a complete wally.' He stopped, flummoxed for a moment. 'Did he say what the name of the place was?'

'I think it's something like the Golden Strand or the Golden Beach Hotel. Something like that.'

'Here, give me the phone directory,' Snake said, starting towards the sitting-room.

'There's no point in ringing him yet,' Mary said. 'He won't be finished until about twenty to twelve and it'll be another half an hour before he stops chatting to the punters. You know him.'

'He'd be finished fucking now, if I got my hands on him,' Snake said, slumping into one of the armchairs in the sitting-room.

'C'mon, relax,' Mary said. 'You'll get him in a while, but you'll have to go out and find a coinbox.'

'Damn!' Snake said, 'I forgot about that. What a pain!'

He reached into his pocket and touched the small packet of speed.

'We might as well give this a kick in the arse while we're waiting,' Snake said, as he placed the small packet on the coffee table.

Snake watched as Mary snorted her line. She wet her fingertip and picked up the tiny traces of greyish white powder that remained.

'Jesus,' Snake said. 'I was horny when I came in a few

minutes ago but you know what this stuff does to me. What'll I be like in another few minutes?'

'That's why I'm smiling,' Mary said. 'We'll soon see who's the horniest.'

Six

The usual last-minute clamour for drink was going on in the lounge of the Golden Strand Hotel. People were standing four deep at the counter, trying to catch the attention of the bartenders. The man with the pear-shaped head and the ill-fitting toupee was red in the face from a combination of heat and effort.

The sides of his head, where he still had his own hair, were dripping with sweat. The toupee had slipped to an even crazier angle than earlier, and even though it remained dry, rivulets of sweat were trickling down his forehead, sliding stingingly into his eyes.

'Can I have a pint of Guinness, a Pernod and white lemonade and a vodka and tonic please?'

Jeannie fingered Danny's ten-pound note as she waited for the drink. She could see him laughing as he approached. Taking the glasses, he led Jeannie out the lounge door and down the corridor to the stairs that led to the bedrooms.

'Where are we going?' Jeannie said, trying to hide the anxiety in her voice.

'I need a smoke. That gig was fucking murder,' he said over his shoulder.

Jeannie followed him up the stairs. Her heart was pounding. It was just herself and Danny. Danny didn't seem to notice her quietness, or if he did, he didn't pretend to. Once inside the room, he locked the door.

'Here's your change,' Jeannie held out the change from the ten-pound note.

Their fingers touched as the money changed hands. Jeannie felt a little charge of electricity as flesh brushed flesh. Danny pocketed his change and filled the pipe quickly. He sucked deeply and offered the pipe to Jeannie.

'I don't know whether I should have any,' Jeannie said. 'I don't really like it.'

The smoke came curling back out of Jeannie's mouth in a blue grey wisp. She looked at Danny and he returned her gaze.

'I think one or both of us should sit down,' said Danny. 'We're like two oul' fellas watching a football match standing the way we are.'

The gaze between them turned to open laughter. As they plonked down on the bed, they giggled for a full thirty seconds. As the giggles died away, Danny looked again at Jeannie and before she could say No, he had reached across and pressed his lips gently on hers. She felt the moist warmth and got a taste of the brown Guinness that flecked the outline of his upper lip.

Jeannie felt Danny's tongue flicking at her lips. The darting flicks were pleasant and, as she relaxed, his tongue slid into her mouth. It was a delicious warm sensation, his tongue licking the sides of her mouth, teasing at her tongue. Her tongue slid into Danny's mouth. He took it in his lips and began to suck. She started to shudder. She felt her nipples getting hard. Danny moved his body, so that his leg was beginning to slide across her thigh. Danny's hand slid to her waist and began to creep up inside the thick sweater. Jeannie felt his warm fingers sliding up her body. His hand moved to cup her breast and just as he closed around it, a loud rap sounded on the door.

'Fuck that,' Danny said softly. 'Yeah?' he called out.

'It's me,' came Sean's voice through the door. 'There's a phone call for you downstairs.'

'Don't go away. I'll be back in a minute,' Danny whispered.

Danny pulled the door behind him, conscious that he still had a bulge in his pants. Sean looked down at it and laughed.

'It's Snake, and he doesn't sound too pleased,' Sean said.

'Snake?' Danny exclaimed. 'How the fuck does he know where we are?'

'Don't ask me.'

They walked down the corridor to the stairs.

'Did you do the business?' Sean asked.

'Just getting into it. She doesn't come on like a veteran and I wouldn't be surprised if she's still a virgin.'

'She's nice all the same,' Sean said.

They reached the bottom of the stairs and Danny walked over and picked up the black handset in the antiquated call-box.

'Snake, my man, what's the Johnny McGory?' Danny said breezily.

'The story is that you're a stupid fucker, doing a stupid cabaret gig for a bunch of stupid fucking rednecks.'

Danny bristled immediately. 'Listen and listen carefully, Snake. I am not a three-year-old and I do not need a lecture from you on how I'm supposed to be living my life.'

'Well, you need a fucking lecture on how to be a professional musician. These stupid gigs in the sticks could blow the whole scam for Poison Pig.'

'Well, I don't exactly see you around to pay the electricity bill on the first of the month, asshole,' Danny spat.

'Yeah, well I was around there at your house tonight, because you were supposed to be doing a session,' Snake countered.

'What do you mean you were around in my house?' Danny snarled.

'I had to call around, because there was no answer from the studio and your fucking phone has been cut off.'

'So Mary told you I was here,' Danny said bitterly.

'She had to, because you fucked up the interview, which I worked so hard to get for weeks now. It's supposed to be at eleven o'clock tomorrow morning in Bewley's and you're down in the arse-end of fucking nowhere.'

'Can't you postpone it?'

'No I can't. If we don't do it now, it'll upset the whole launch of the band.'

'Yeah, well keep your hair on. We'll be there.'

'And don't be late,' Snake snapped.

'Fuck off,' Danny shouted, banging the phone down on the cradle. 'Slithery little bastard.'

*   *   *

It was 2am when Snake O'Reilly left Danny Toner's house in Reginald Street. The streets were quiet and he could hear his own footsteps echoing on the pavement as he walked to his car. The warm night air brought a stillness and calm to the city. Just minutes earlier he had been on the point of sleep, lying beside Mary Toner, but now Snake was wide awake and the speed was re-asserting itself in his system. If Frankie was true to form, Snake thought, there was a good chance that he would be in Suesey Street, the night club at the top of the Leeson Street strip. He nosed the car onto Pembroke Street, found a parking spot and quickly descended to the basement club. He let his eyes adjust to the gloom. Across the bar he could see Frankie in animated conversation with a well-known publicist from the record business. Snake pushed his way through the crowd and came to Frankie's shoulder.

'How would you two boys like to join a band?' Snake laughed.

'How's it going, Snake?' Frankie said.

'Did nobody tell these people there's a recession?' Snake joked.

'I can't even spell recession, what's your excuse?' Frankie laughed. 'Will you have a glass?' He offered the bottle of Muscadet to Snake.

Snake looked disapprovingly at the bottle of wine and snapped his fingers at the girl behind the bar.

'Can I have a bottle of Charles Heidesieck?' He pulled a wad of notes from his pocket and ostentatiously waved it around as he waited for his bottle of champagne. He checked to see if he was making an impression, but no one appeared to be taking any notice of him.

'Where were you till now?' Frankie asked.

'Just taking care of a bit of business,' Snake said.

'Anyone we know?' Frankie leered.

'Is that all you ever think about?' Snake said, wondering if there was any threatening innuendo in Frankie's remark.

'I also think about drink and drugs and rock 'n' roll,' retorted Frankie, 'but I have to confess, getting laid is top of the list.'

'You're cool for the interview in the morning?' Snake asked.

'I'm always cool,' Frankie smiled.

'Yeah, well don't get too fucked up on drink tonight,' laughed Snake. 'We'll need your brain in the morning.'

Frankie gave a loud guffaw.

'How are the rehearsals going?' Snake continued.

'Good, very good. The sound is great and I think we're all much more relaxed with each other now,' Frankie answered.

'How are you finding Danny?'

'He's a bit of a know-all prick at times,' Frankie said. 'But he's a good singer and he's a great poser.'

'How about Sean?'

'Sean is cool. He doesn't say much but he's a terrific drummer. I have great confidence in him. It's brilliant when you don't have to worry about the drummer. I've been in bands with some really poxy drummers and it's desperate.'

Snake was now getting to the real purpose of his probing.

'Richie plays very well with Sean, doesn't he?'

'Brilliant. He's a brilliant player. I'll tell you something, Snake, we're a fucking good band. Best band I've ever been in.'

'Richie's very quiet though, isn't he?' Snake said, again leaving the question hanging in the air.

'Ah, I don't know. He's a quiet bloke,' said Frankie. 'Why?'

'I just thought he's been quieter than ever lately, y'know,' Snake said.

'Yeah, well, since his mother died, I think not having her around has affected him badly,' Frankie said.

'Well that's just it, I'd be worried that it might be getting in on him and I wouldn't like it to get any worse, especially because of what he went through in the past.'

'You mean being an addict?' Frankie asked.

'Yeah. Does he ever talk about it?'

'Not really. I asked him about it once and he told me he spent a bit of time in some centre. But he's clean now.'

'How do you know?' Snake asked.

''Cos I've been around a lot of junkies and you know when someone is on smack, especially when they're strung out on it.'

'Yeah. Well, just keep an eye on him for me. I'd hate for him to fall off the wagon.'

Seven

It was nine o'clock in the morning when the battered yellow Citroen Dyane reached Newlands Cross. Behind the wheel, Danny Toner had a manic grin on his face. He threw a quick look into the rear-view mirror and saw the reflection of his bloodshot eyes. Sliding the window on the driver's side forward, he stuck his head out and roared at the surrounding traffic.

'Look out, ol' red eyes is back.'

'Bear left, bear right and bear straight on,' Sean laughed. 'Am I right, Jeannie?'

'I don't know where I am, so I'll just have to trust you two,' she giggled in reply.

The traffic began to thicken as they reached the north quays.

'Dear Jesus,' Danny sighed, 'this is the only country in the world where the morning rush hour starts at nine o'clock. In any other civilised country in the world, people are at their work hours ago. No wonder this country is fucked.'

'What's more, these dumb bastards are getting in the way of us superstars trying to get to our important interview, so that we can tell the world how we feel about our favourite food and our favourite film stars,' Sean laughed.

'We did well all the same,' continued Danny. 'What time did we leave the Golden Strand, l-u-x-u-r-y hotel.'

'I haven't a clue,' Sean responded. 'What time was it Jeannie, when we left?'

'I think it was about a quarter to six,' Jeannie said.

'Sure we flew here,' Danny cackled. 'Did we leave out anywhere on the way?'

Danny's red eyes were the end product of a full night's drinking, several pipes of hash and a total lack of sleep. Sean was a bit rheumy-eyed as well. Jeannie looked the freshest of the three of them, having had less to drink than the others.

Danny was getting exasperated with the traffic.

'Little old ladies of both fucking sexes. Where in the name of Jaysus do they come from.'

He reached into his shirt pocket. He removed his small brass pipe and the box of matches, which contained the significantly smaller lump of hash.

'Turf patrol?'

Sean nodded, taking the pipe and the box. The bowl of hash took the edge off Danny's agitation.

'What time is it?' he asked.

'Don't know,' came the reply in unison from Sean and Jeannie.

Danny slid the window forward and looked into the car on his right in the three-abreast, solid mass of cars and buses.

Two girls, fresh and ready for a day at the office, stared in wonderment at the bleary-eyed vagabond with the stubbly chin and the cheeky grin. The girl in the passenger seat rolled down the window at Danny's behest.

'Excuse me, but what time is it?' Danny asked, taking care to articulate every word.

The bright-eyed girl could smell the Pernod, even across the two feet between the cars.

'It's 9.29,' she answered, glancing at her watch.

'I have one further question for you, if that's all right?'

'OK,' she said.

'What day is it – and where am I?'

'That's two,' the girl smiled.

'Who's counting?' laughed Danny. 'Thank you for your divine assistance.'

He slid the window closed again and turned to Sean and Jeannie. 'Chaps and chapesses, this is a pain in the arse. Sean, slide that window forward there and stick your left paw out.

We're going to cut across these mother-fuckers and go up to the markets where we can get a civilised drink.'

*   *   *

Snake O'Reilly looked up from a table in the corner, as he heard the loud laughter. Frankie and Richie sat opposite him. Beside him was the writer from *Hot Press*. Snake was consulting his watch anxiously for the fifth time when he heard the commotion. He looked across to the entrance. Danny came in, one arm around Sean's shoulders, his other around a young girl Snake had never seen before. He took his left arm from around the girl's shoulder, extended it in front of him and, like General Custer leading a cavalry charge, he ran towards them.

'There they are!' he shouted.

With his arm outstretched before him, half-dragging Sean along behind him, Danny threaded his way to them, laughing uproariously.

'Sweet Jesus,' muttered Snake under his breath, throwing a glance to see how the journalist was reacting. The journalist had an amused grin on his face.

'Good morning, brethren,' Danny said, a lugubrious smile creasing his face. 'May we present Miss Jeannie Callanan from the Arse-End-of-Nowhere.'

Jeannie smiled a shy smile at the table's occupants. Snake was conscious that the whole café had turned to look at the spectacle of the two loud drunks with the slip of a girl, who had come clumping in, destroying the muted tranquillity of the coffee house.

'So where did you two manage to get into such a condition?'

'My good man,' Danny said, drawing himself up to his full height, straightening Sean up beside him. 'This man and I spent a hot and sweaty night pouring out our creative juices in a hot and sweaty recording studio, while our fellow men flittered away their hours on this earth in futile pursuits such as sleep. As dawn broke, we felt the Muse deserved some liquid reward for a night of great endeavour, so we went to the markets and got pissed.'

Everybody at the table laughed. Snake looked to see that the writer was laughing with the rest.

'Snake, my man,' Danny said, leaning down and chucking Snake under the chin with his fingers. 'You are a terrible worrier.'

*   *   *

'I thought Snake was going to have a shit haemorrhage when you walked in,' Frankie said, after Snake and the journalist had left.

'Smarten his hump for him,' Sean said.

'I'll tell you something. I'm knackered now,' Danny interjected. 'I think I'd better get to the scratcher before I capsize here.'

'You do that,' Frankie said. 'You look like you need it.'

Danny turned to Jeannie. 'OK, babe, can you ring your aunt or do you know where she lives or whatever and we'll get you home first.'

Jeannie had been dreading this moment from the minute they had arrived in Dublin.

She leaned closer and whispered to Danny, 'Can I talk to you privately for a minute?'

'Yeah sure, let's go out to the door there.'

They got up from the table and walked towards the door.

'So, what's the problem?'

'I didn't quite tell you the truth,' Jeannie whispered, her eyes fixed on the ground.

'What do you mean exactly?'

'I don't have any aunt in Dublin to go to. When I met you yesterday, I was running away from home.'

'Aw, for fuck's sake,' Danny said, throwing his eyes to heaven. 'And why are you running away from home?'

'It would take a while to tell you,' she said sheepishly.

'And did you lie about your age as well?'

'I did last night when I told you I was eighteen, but today is my birthday and I swear I'm eighteen today. I have my birth certificate in the car. I'll show it to you.'

'No, no. It's OK, I believe you,' Danny said, trying to deal with this sudden turn of events. He was starting to come down off the drink and the dope, and tiredness was weighing heavily on his eyelids.

He looked at Jeannie. Her eyes seemed to have swollen to twice their size and she looked as though tears were not far away.

'So what you're trying to tell me is that you have nowhere to stay?'

'Could I stay with you just for tonight?' she asked shyly.

Danny dropped his eyes to the floor momentarily. 'Jeannie, I didn't exactly tell you the whole story last night either.'

'What do you mean?'

'I'm married,' he said, raising his gaze to meet hers.

'You're married,' she said incredulously.

'I have two kids, a boy and a girl, and I live at home with my wife Mary.'

'And what about last night, when you were kissing me and everything?'

'Well, to tell you the truth, it was just a bit of rock 'n' roll fun when it started out, but then I realised that you are probably still a virgin. Am I right?'

Jeannie blushed bright red.

'Anyway, I decided to back off,' Danny continued. 'And if

45

the truth were known, I enjoyed your company right until this minute.'

'And if you had made love to me last night, would you have just dumped me then?' she asked, trying to blink back the tears.

'All I can say to you honestly is that last night was last night. Now we've shared a bit of an experience and I was hoping that you would go on being my friend.'

'But how can you be my friend if you're married?'

'Listen, just because I'm married doesn't mean I can't be a friend.'

A tear slid down Jeannie's cheek. Danny reached out and put his hand on hers and squeezed gently.

'Keep calm for a minute. I'm bollocksed now and I can hardly think straight, but we'll get you fixed up now for today and I'll talk to you later when I've had a few hours' sleep myself. Just let me have a chat with Sean.'

Jeannie watched as Danny walked to the others and began talking to Sean. He came back to her, a reassuring look in his eyes.

'OK, everything's cool. You can go home with Sean now and get a few hours' sleep on his couch. Later we'll work out what you can do. Is that all right?'

'Yes,' she said quietly.

Danny reached out and wiped away the tear from her cheek.

'You're a really nice person,' he smiled at her.

She smiled back at him through the tears. 'Thanks.'

'Happy birthday, Jeannie.'

*   *   *

The *Hot Press* interview helped enormously in getting the band attention. 'STOP THE BULLSHIT' the heading read. The writer had obviously been sympathetic to the mood of the morning in Bewley's. He had gently probed Danny's background, only to be quickly rebuffed.

'Like everything else, my background is bullshit,' Danny told him. 'I keep listening to people like Bono talking about unemployment and what we must do about it. Bruce Springsteen gives a thousand pounds here or there to some local charity, but it's all bullshit. They're not giving something back because of some great philosophy or deep commitment they have had all their lives. Springsteen is from some poxy little place in New Jersey, and if he hadn't become a star, he would probably have wound up sitting with a bunch of no-hope working-class men, sipping beer in some lousy joint in Asbury Park.

'Then you've Sting off saving the rainforest. Fair play to him and what a great guy he is, but when the monsoon comes you can bet your arse Sting will head for a hammock somewhere the sun is shining and he'll get back to saving the forest when the weather improves.

'The same goes for Bono. He's just a middle-class boy who was a Mr Clean. Luckily for him, that was a good image and he was sincere about it and that shone through. But his experience and his philosophy now is the philosophy of someone who is at the highest level of rock stardom and he doesn't have any real contact with anybody except other rock stars and people in the business.

'Sure he goes stomping around Sellafield in wellingtons and a gas mask, but will that close Sellafield or sway British politicians to change their nuclear policies? I don't think so, and Bono and the lads should wise up and get on with the music. It's too easy to excite an audience of eighty thousand for an hour and think that you are doing something for mankind. And most rock stars are not even as bright as Bono. Most of them are gobshites.

'And something else that is *very* important. We are not The Commitments. We didn't start this band to escape from our working-class ghetto into a land of limos, so we don't need to do any "glamour" shots against burning fires and walls with graffiti. Every record company that comes here is looking for another band with a hard luck story. Fuck that.

'The point I'm trying to make is that all that matters is what I am now. And right now I am trying to just be me, as I am today, singing music for the sake of the music and not for Nelson Mandela or some other terrorist in jail in Chile. I can't do a fucking thing for the starving with my songs and this band won't help anybody get out of jail. Why go through all the bullshit? I preferred Geldof when he wanted to get rich and get laid.'

The attack on Bono, Sting, Springsteen and Geldof caused a great rumpus in the papers. Every craw-thumper on every newspaper slammed Poison Pig, and Danny in particular. The band was dismissed as a bunch of foul-mouthed louts, who had no consideration for their fellow human beings. One columnist wrote, 'It is mindless twerps like Poison Pig who still give rock music a bad name.'

Flushed with success, Snake hustled hard to get on 'The Late Late Show'. An appearance there would reach a huge audience. Snake pestered one of the researchers until she finally came to the Baggot Inn to see what all the fuss was about. She was impressed by the band, especially by Danny.

'OK,' she said. 'I'll ring you with a date. But no funny business when you come on.'

'No funny business,' Snake laughed.

Eight

Danny found himself sitting bolt upright in bed, wide awake. He didn't know whether he had woken first or sat up first. He tried to recall what he had been dreaming about at the instant he had woken, but his memory gave him a mocking glimpse of the final scene and the image slipped away. Mary stirred and Danny turned to look at her. She looked very beautiful lying there, her face serene and relaxed, her skin without a hint of blemish. Mary's face was clean of all traces of make-up and the perfect symmetrical curves of her high prominent cheekbones drew his eyes to the full lips, warm and soft.

Danny remembered how he used to say to her, 'You have the kind of lips that they draw on girls in True Romance comics.' In the beginning, Mary had thought he was criticising her lips. She would get hurt and Danny would tease her mercilessly and then as time went on she had realised he really liked the way her lips looked.

Kissing Mary had been such a thrill for Danny. His own full lips pressed on Mary's perfect mouth had been a truly sensuous experience. Sometimes he would kiss her for hours, teasing out the kisses for as long as ten minutes. Once they held one kiss for an hour, slavering through the final minutes, watching a clock beside the bed, stripping each other slowly of clothing as the sixty-minute mark approached. They had stroked each other's bodies, teasing, arousing, titillating, caressing along each other's calves, hands flicking gently at nipples, till they made fierce and frantic love, as the minute hand reached the hour.

Mary's kisses didn't excite Danny that way any more. He looked at her and knew in his heart that he still loved her, but their lovemaking had become perfunctory and the slow build-up of kisses had long since been abandoned.

Danny wondered if Mary missed the excitement too. He remembered how she had taken the initiative lots of times sliding her hand down along his belly as they had lain in bed. It had been a long time since she had last done that.

Guilt was stirring in Danny's mind. The night before, he had finally made love to Jeannie Callanan, six weeks to the day from their meeting outside the Golden Strand Hotel. In the six weeks that had passed, Danny had seen Jeannie every single day.

Jeannie was now sharing Richie Killen's two-bedroomed flat. The second bedroom was tiny, but it suited the purpose perfectly. Danny had had to use all his charm and persuasive powers to get Richie to agree to let Jeannie share.

'I need my own space, Danny,' Richie told him.

'Listen, Richie, it'll only be for a little while. She's a really nice girl and she'll be a bit of company, not that you'll see much of her now that we're starting into the serious stage of our rehearsals. Put yourself in her shoes, man. Wouldn't you be glad of it if someone did it for your sister?'

Since then, Danny had contrived reasons to ring the house or call to it. He had looked forward to seeing Jeannie every day and now with rehearsals, the gigs, the interviews and the controversy, Danny had plenty of excuses to be absent from home for hours.

He had been kissing Jeannie from her first night in Dublin. It had started as a friendly full peck to begin with, until the day she had landed a job as a waitress with Danny's help.

'Thanks for getting me the job.'

'It's nothing.' Danny tried to shrug it off. 'I just hope you like it and that you make some bread at it. Have you ever waited on tables before?'

'Not really.'

'It'll be cool. You'll learn fast enough. You're a bright little bastard.'

'Thanks a lot,' Jeannie said, affecting an offended air.

'Joke, joke.'

He leaned down to kiss her. The lips touched just a tiny fraction of a second longer than the usual peck, just enough to tip them over the edge, to a full soft kiss.

'I'll see you tomorrow,' she whispered, as their mouths drew apart.

'Yeah,' he replied, hearing his own voice echoing hollowly inside his head.

Inevitably the kissing had grown more intense, but in the end it was drink rather than Danny's charm that had finally relaxed Jeannie enough to make love.

'Did you come?' Danny asked.

'I don't really know.'

'Well, what was the sensation like?'

'It was like my body was ...' she groped for some comparison that would describe the feeling. 'As if my body was reaching up for something and I was nearly reaching it, but I never got there.'

'I got bad news for you,' Danny laughed. 'I don't think you came.'

'Is there something wrong with me?'

'Not at all.' Danny curbed his laughter, sensing Jeannie's genuine anxiety. 'Some women never have orgasms. Some women have a thing called multiple orgasm. Some women come all the time. And some women only come some of the time. And like everything else in life, there are no real rules. Next time I'll try and make sure you touch whatever it is you're reaching for.'

*　　*　　*

Danny slid his legs out of bed and winced. The pain above his eyes stabbed at him as soon as he stood. He and Jeannie had polished off a bottle of vodka between them in Jeannie's flat the night before. It must have been five o'clock at least when he got home.

Danny reached the return on the stairs and stopped and looked down at the pile of letters on the hall floor. Three brown ones and four white ones lay in a jumbled pile.

'Jaysus, the good guys won by one today,' he muttered to himself, as he took the last few steps and picked up the mail.

He walked into the kitchen, flicking through the letters as he went. Two of the brown envelopes contained parking tickets. One had a circular about a sale of work in aid of the Catholic Boy Scouts of Ireland. The last brown envelope was from the television rental company.

Danny slit open one of the white envelopes. He pulled out a sheet of white paper that had been folded over three times.

'Bono and Geldof are saints. Poison Pig are scumbags. We'll get you.'

Danny examined the sheet of paper. It was unsigned, and there was no clue as to where it might have come from. He turned over the envelope and looked at the postmark. He shrugged and put the letter down. Flicking on the switch of the electric kettle, Danny reached for the jar of coffee on the shelf beside the cooker. When the kettle had boiled he made himself a cup of coffee, putting in three heaped spoons of sugar. He sat down at the table and picked up the anonymous letter again.

'You'll love this, Snake,' he said out loud.

The phone rang and Danny sprang to pick it up. He didn't want Mary to wake.

'Hello.'

'Danny, Snake here. What's happening?'

'Not much. I'm just up.'

'How did last night go?'

'Last night was fine.'

'Good stuff,' sneered Snake. 'Nothing like getting your teeth into something fresh.'

'What the fuck's the matter with you?' Danny asked.

Danny knew Snake was aware that he was seeing Jeannie a lot. It didn't bother him, but in his high state of panicky guilt at the happenings of the night before, everything sounded like a threat of exposure.

'There's nothing wrong with me,' Snake said. 'I was merely saying that it must be good to be working on new material.'

'Yeah, yeah, very satisfying.'

'Are you coming into the office today?' Snake asked. 'I have a few letters you'll be very interested to see.'

'And I have a very interesting letter for you too,' Danny said.

'What time will you be in?'

'I'll leave now, so I suppose in about fifteen minutes.'

'Make it half an hour. And by the way, buy yourself a copy of *Hot Press*. I think you'll like the review we got for last week's gig.'

'I'd forgotten about that. OK. See you in a while.'

Danny replaced the receiver, put the letter in his pocket and ran lightly back up the stairs, ignoring the staccato stabs of pain in his head that came with every step.

'I'm needed in the office,' he said to Mary quietly, hoping not to waken her fully. 'I'll give you a buzz later.'

He swung the car into Meath Street and stopped at a newsagent's. The *Hot Press* cover had Bono staring moodily into space.

'Prophetic,' Danny said.

He sat in the car and read the review.

Nine

Snake had twenty photocopies of the review on his desk when Danny walked in.

'Some review, huh?'

'Unbelievable,' Danny laughed. 'Whatever about being stuffed for the last two weeks, what the fuck is it going to be like tonight at the Baggot Inn?'

'I think we'll be able to up the cover charge by a pound a skull next week,' Snake said, gleefully rubbing his hands together. 'But it's not this money. This money from the gig is piddle-arse money. All the signs are there that we might be on the trail of the real stuff.'

'This might help us even more,' Danny said, producing the threatening letter from his pocket.

Snake took the letter and read it, a soft whistle escaping from his lips.

'Are you scared about it?'

'Scared, me arse. I think it's fucking great. I hope I get millions of them. You said you wanted me to be controversial. Well, here we go, here we go, here we go.'

'Hey, I'm the ideas man around here,' Snake chided playfully.

'We should get a few of our family to send us a few more and blow it up into a story in the papers.'

'Well, wait till you see my letters.' Snake tossed a sheet of paper across the desk to Danny.

He started to read.

As a concerned parent who is trying to raise two teenage boys and a teenage girl in these troubled times, I am outraged by the behaviour of your band Poison Pig.

It is disgraceful to see obscenity portrayed in such a

glamorous light in this Catholic country. It is against all of the ideals that the Pope preached to the young people of Ireland and to allow your band to go on corrupting the minds of our youth is irresponsible and sinful in the eyes of God.

Bob Geldof and Bono are the best example Irish youth have ever had and God will judge them for the great good they are doing for humanity. The attack on them is nothing short of a pagan disgrace.

Call off your filthy hounds before it is too late.'

'Is this for real or is it a piss-take?' Danny laughed.

'I thought it might be a piss-take,' Snake answered. 'But read the other two letters. They are basically saying the same thing without being as hysterical.'

'Jaysus, we really got under their skin didn't we?'

A knock at the door signalled the arrival of Sean, a copy of *Hot Press* stuck conspicuously in his jacket pocket.

'I see it says in here that the drummer with this new band Poison Pig is really hot stuff. I wonder if he would like to meet me,' he smirked.

'What about it?' Danny laughed. 'Aren't we impressed with us?'

'I'll tell you one thing though, I'm taking some terrible stick from my family about the band.'

'What do you mean, Sean?'

'They're givin' out to me about slagging Geldof and Bono. They all think these guys are fucking saints. I told my aunt they would have to crucify them in stereo, one on the left, one on the right. She told me I'd go to hell for blasphemy.'

Snake looked ecstatic.

'I'm telling you, Danny, we're onto something hot. We need to do something else completely outrageous, just to clinch it. Slagging Bono and Geldof is great, but one more thing would clinch it. Just one more.'

'What about the "Late Late"?' Danny said quietly.

'What about it?'

'Why don't we pull a major on the "Late Late Show"?'

'I thought they told us no funny business,' Sean interjected.

'Hold it, hold it,' Snake said. 'Carry on, Danny, what were you thinking about?'

'I dunno. Some stunt. If we had some stunt, just at the end of the song. Or even better, in the middle. Get them to black us out. Jaysus, that's it. For fuck's sake. No one has ever been blacked out on the "Late Late".'

Snake's eyes were ablaze with enthusiasm.

'You could hide a T-shirt under some kind of a jacket, or under a shirt with one of those Velcro strips that tear open.'

'I have it, I have it', Sean whooped. '"Bono Fucks Dead Midgets" on the T-shirt.'

'Great, great,' chortled Danny. 'How about a photo of a Somalian with the caption "Geldof ate my lunch"?'

'Go 'way, you pussycat,' Sean jeered. 'That's too bleedin' tame. It'll have to be raunchy. What about "Fuck Nelson Mandela, I'm with Chuck Berry."?'

'You're right,' Snake agreed. 'It'll have to be really rude.'

'Should we go with "Fuck the World" to hammer home the message?' Danny asked.

'I hear what you're saying,' Snake answered. 'But I think Sean has the right idea.'

'"Course I have,' Sean laughed. 'Sure amn't I a bright bollocks altogether?'

'Have you got the demo of "Designer Aid"?' Snake asked.

'Right here in my pocket,' Sean said. He produced a cassette and stuck it in the machine that sat on the shelf up behind Snake's head. A big booming guitar came shimmering out through the speakers.

'You don't have to ask where we robbed that riff,' Danny

chuckled.

'Designer Aid' was powerful.

> *Would you like to eat my Gucci shoes?*
> *Would you like to touch my hair?*
> *On a continent where fashion has no God,*
> *Let me wander darkly through this Third World*
> *Rock 'n' roll affair*
> *Where contrast mocks a world that's truly odd*
>
> *Designer Aid*
>
> *We put hipness in your hunger*
> *Designer Aid*
> *Designer Aid*
> *Designer Aid*
> *My Armani suit will fit somebody*
> *Get some photographs*
> *We'll use them on the next album sleeve*
> *Champagne and rice, the opposites*
> *communion passes round*
> *Skinny models make them feel at ease*
>
> *Designer Aid*
> *Hipness in your hunger*
> *Designer Aid*
> *Hipness in your hunger*
> *Designer Aid*
> *Designer Aid*
> *Oh, oh, oh, oh, oh, oh, oh*

'Fuck me, that's powerful,' Danny said. 'Frankie really got a great guitar sound. I think we should do this one on the television.'

'Well, I have a confession to make, I already told them that you were going to sing "Designer Aid". I had a feeling about this one that it was goin' to be just right,' Snake said. 'I think we should release it as a single.'

'When are we doing the show? Two weeks away is it?' Danny asked.

Snake nodded affirmatively. Inside he was seething. His only miscalculation had been his strategy on a single. He had aimed at attracting the record companies from England and America without having to release a record. Now, seeing the response and feedback, Snake knew a single would do well.

'We'd need to go in and do it tomorrow if you want to have it out in two weeks. Am I right, Snake?' Sean said.

'Sean is right,' Snake agreed. 'Ten days. It can be done in a week, but it's always dodgy.'

'Let's go for it,' Danny said. 'The Baggot gigs will pay for it, and we're bound to get more gigs out of it.'

'Where would you do it?' Snake asked.

'I'll find an available studio,' Sean said.

'That means no piss-up tonight,' Danny said.

'There'll be plenty other piss-ups,' Snake said quietly.

Ten

Danny had warned Jeannie to be early for the gig in the Baggot Inn.

'After the review in *Hot Press*, the place is going to be black tonight, completely mobbed. I'll have you on the guest list with three stars after your name. Are you going to bring someone with you?'

'I'm bringing Myra, one of the girls who works with me.'

'All right. Hang around and wait for me afterwards. I won't

have a chance to talk to you beforehand.'

'OK, I hope the gig goes well.'

'With you there, how can it fail?'

As Jeannie and Myra turned the corner of Merrion Row, they could see that a line of people had already formed outside the Baggot Inn and was stretching twenty yards back down the street. Several drinkers from Doheny and Nesbitt's pub across the street from the Baggot had taken their pints onto the footpath to watch the build-up of people.

'Will we have to stand around until this mob get in?' Myra asked.

Jeannie was hesitant. 'I'm not really sure. Danny told me just to walk straight up to the door.'

The two of them stood indecisively, Jeannie hoping she might see a familiar face connected with the band.

'What time is it?' Jeannie asked.

'It must be close to nine o'clock.'

'I wonder what time they'll start letting people in?'

'Why don't we just walk across and see what the situation is?' Myra suggested.

'You're right,' Jeannie said.

'C'mon,' Myra said. 'Otherwise we'll be out here all night.'

Jeannie was a little bit flustered as she got to the door. It was shut firmly. She knocked timidly and it opened a fraction of an inch.

'I'm on the guest list,' Jeannie whispered, as quietly as possible.

'What's your name?' the doorman bellowed.

'Jeannie Callanan.'

'Hold on.'

The door opened just enough to permit Jeannie to walk through. 'Callanan by two,' he said. 'Where's your other one?'

Jeannie reached back and pulled at Myra's sleeve, tugging her in behind her. It was only when they got through the door that Jeannie realised that the bar was already full. An Elvis Costello tape was booming through the speakers and there was a general air of excitement and expectancy. Jeannie felt a hand on her shoulder. She looked around. Richie was standing there, a big smile on his face.

'Some crowd, eh?'

'It certainly is,' Jeannie replied. 'This is my friend Myra.'

Richie shook hands with Myra. 'I have to head on down to the lads. Might see you later, I hope.'

'See ya,' Jeannie said.

'He's nice,' Myra said, as Richie fought his way through the crowd.

'Yes, he is,' Jeannie said. 'He's a really nice guy. Very gentle.'

'That's the guy you share the flat with, isn't it?'

'Yeah, but there's nothing like that in it,' Jeannie said quickly. 'We're just good pals.'

*   *   *

Myra volunteered to buy the first drink. As she stood at the back waiting, Jeannie thought about the way Richie had looked at her in the past week. She was conscious that several times she had caught him staring at her intently, even when they had been just sitting around at home in the flat.

When Danny had first persuaded Richie to let Jeannie take the second bedroom, Richie had been extremely moody. He had only spoken to Jeannie when she had addressed him. More often than not, he had stayed in his bedroom if Jeannie was around, or else he had waited until Jeannie was in her bedroom and then he would sit in the living-room, watching television, reading or listening to the radio.

Gradually he had started to loosen up. He had begun to talk to Jeannie, asking her about her work. They had compared their favourite bands and singers, and the tension had eased considerably. Danny had told Jeannie about Richie's heroin addiction and how he had come to be living in a flat on his own, after the death of his mother.

'Do you miss living at home?' Jeannie asked him one night.

Richie looked at her guardedly. 'What do you mean?'

'I don't mean anything other than do you miss home. I don't know if Danny told you, but I was running away from home when I met him.'

'Why were you running away? Danny has never explained to me fully.'

Jeannie told Richie her story. He listened attentively.

'I still sometimes miss the smell of home and the smell of my own room,' she said.

'I know what you mean,' Richie said. 'I'm sorry for snapping at you. I do miss home. I miss my brother and my sisters. And most of all I miss my mother.'

Richie looked at Jeannie, searching her face with his eyes, as if to make sure that her concern and interest in him was genuine. Then he told his own story quietly and unemotionally.

'So, my mother was the one who pulled me through two overdoses. And she stopped my Da from picking on me all the time. I hit him once, when he gave me a thump and after that I knew I had to get out.'

'And do you go home now at all?'

'Yeah. In the afternoons when the kids get home from school, or else I meet them somewhere.'

'What do they think of you being in the band?'

'Brilliant. I'm going to try and sneak my brother into the gig, but if my Da found out there'd be war.'

'Do you never talk to him at all?'

'Not for weeks. He rang me to talk about Mam but he couldn't talk about her without shouting ...'

Richie broke down in tears. Jeannie took him in her arms and felt him heave as huge sobs wracked his body. She stroked his hair tenderly until the crying subsided.

'Sorry about that,' Richie said as he wiped his eyes. 'I don't know whether I'm crying for me or my Da. I feel so sorry for him, but I can't help him because he won't let me.'

'A bit like my own father,' Jeannie said. 'How did you ever get into heroin in the first place?' she added.

'A girl,' Richie answered, with a rueful smile. 'My first year in art college. She was two years older than me and it was so cool at the time. She showed me how to smoke it.'

'I thought addicts injected it?'

'That came later. I moved into a house with her and four other people from college and things just got very sloppy.'

'And why did you try to take an overdose?'

'Just part of the trip.' He fell silent, as if reliving the feeling mentally.

'I'd prefer not to talk about it any more. It's just ...'

'It's OK,' Jeannie said, 'I understand.'

After baring their souls to one another, Richie and Jeannie became firm friends. Richie genuinely seemed to lighten up, joking and laughing in a way that was new to Jeannie. When Danny called, Richie would excuse himself after a few minutes of chit-chat and retire to his bedroom.

Then just a few days before the Baggot Inn gig, Richie levelled his gaze at Jeannie, trapping her eyes so that she could not look away.

'Are you and Danny having a scene?'

For an instant Jeannie was flustered.

'Danny has just been very good to me. He likes me and I like him and we're good friends. If it wasn't for Danny, I don't know what I would have done when I got to Dublin.'

'Have you met his wife yet?'

'Not really. I saw her at a gig and she was in this restaurant with the kids one day, but I didn't talk to her. She's beautiful, isn't she?'

Richie did not answer.

'Why are you asking all these questions, Richie?'

'I was just wondering. That's all. Would you like to go to a movie?'

Warning bells began to ring in Jeannie's brain. She hadn't been imagining things. Richie had grown more attentive and more direct. The questions about Danny, the way she kept catching him looking at her and now the invitation to the pictures, it all seemed to add up.

'When do you want to go to the movies?'

'Right now,' Richie said.

She hesitated for a moment. Richie held her gaze firmly.

'Why not?' she said. 'Just give me a minute to stick on a bit of make-up and I'll be right with you.'

'You look beautiful enough without it,' Richie smiled.

Eleven

'What is Poison Pig's music like really?' Myra asked, as she returned with a drink for Jeannie. 'I know you told me it's a bit like U2, but is it a rip-off of U2?'

'Well, the sound is a bit like U2, but the idea is that they're against the way U2 and Bob Geldof and all those other rock stars are getting involved in politics and in stuff like that.'

'D'you like the music?' Myra asked.

'I wasn't into this kind of music before, but Danny played me a lot of the demo tapes they made and I know some of the songs a bit now and I'm getting to like it. Danny is brilliant on stage.'

A sudden buzz indicated the first bodies on stage. Sean was

in behind the drums, kicking the bass drum. Richie was plugging in his bass and on the right-hand side of the stage Frankie had plugged in his guitar and was fiddling with the volume control knobs on it.

There was a buzz of expectancy from the crowd. A guitar chord burst from the speakers, the echo swirling through the darkened room. Three flash pans, set up in front of the band, exploded. Sean kicked the bass drum four times, counting in the band and then with lights flashing through, green, red, orange, white and blue, Poison Pig drove into the opening bars of 'RIP – The World'.

Sean, Richie and Frankie were dressed in black, each in his own individual style. Sean had a black bomber jacket in silk. Frankie's suit had huge broad shoulders and pants that ballooned out from the waist and gathered in tight again, just above the ankle. Richie was sporting a black Chinese mandarin jacket.

Each of them had dyed their hair a black-blue colour. Sean's had been back-combed into a pompadour. Frankie's had been shaved around the bottom, leaving a clean swathe running about two inches all around his head. Another two inches of black hair sat in a wedge on top. Richie's curls were even more dramatic, now that they had been dyed jet-black.

'They look great, if nothing else,' Myra shouted.

Jeannie scarcely heard her. She was watching for Danny's entrance. A roar went up as he came running through the crowd. He weaved his way through the stools and tables and bounced onto the stage. Grabbing the microphone in his hand, Danny whirled and pointed his finger like a claw at the people at the front tables.

He began to sing:

> *Your time is nearly over*
> *That is what they tell you if you let them into your brain*

But I can save you now
Get this junkie off your shoulder
Follow me, I'll lead you to a place that has no pain
Follow me
Follow me ...

Jeannie hadn't seen Danny with his new dyed jet-black hair. It stood up like a crown, cut in small arcs that swept up to little peaks all around his head. Jeannie could see that he had used black eye-liner and a spot of rouge on his cheeks.

His powerful voice cut through the sound of the instruments. In his black undertaker's coat, with the Devil's head brooch hanging outside, Danny looked menacing until he smiled, and then the full mischief of Poison Pig seemed to flow out over the crowd:

RIP for the serious men
RIP for the serious men
We hope we never see their likes again ...

For the next forty-five minutes, Danny was in full control of his audience, whirling and pointing, urging the dancing audience on, jumping in amongst them, singing the long chanting chorus.

'This is going to be our new single,' Danny roared. 'It's called "Designer Aid". Buy it.'

Would you like to wear my Gucci shoes?
Would you like to touch my hair? ...

Thunderous applause greeted the end of 'Designer Aid'. Danny sprinted off the stage with Sean, Frankie and Richie following him. In the dressing-room they heard the crowd yelling for more and stomping their feet.

'Take your time, take your time,' Snake said to Danny. 'Let them sweat a bit.'

'Yeah, but we don't want to blow it by being too cool either,' Danny shouted.

'All right. Go now,' Snake said.

The band ran back on stage and played a two-song encore. After a full five minutes of chanting and banging bottles on tables, the crowd reluctantly acknowledged that the gig was over and began to trickle out the door into Baggot Street.

Jeannie and Myra sat down, relieved to get a seat at last.

'Well, what did you think?' Jeannie asked.

'Brilliant,' Myra answered. 'Absolutely great. Danny is amazingly good and the rest of the band is brilliant too.'

They sat for quite a while watching as various rock luminaries who had gone backstage to talk to the band passed them by. Eventually Snake appeared around the corner from the dressing-room. He spotted Jeannie.

'Hi ya, Jeannie. Do you want to go on back?'

'Is it all right now?' Jeannie asked.

'Yeah, it's cool,' Snake said.

'This is Myra.'

Jeannie led Myra down through the pub and up the stairs to the dressing-room. She knocked timidly. Frankie opened the door.

'Hello there, Jeannie, come in,' he said.

'Hello, Danny,' Jeannie smiled.

'What did you think?'

'Brilliant. Both of us thought it was brilliant. This is Myra.'

'I like your friend,' Sean whispered in her ear, as he passed her, heading for the door.

'Where are you off to, Sean?' Danny asked.

'A long slow pony,' laughed Sean. 'Yer only man after a gig.'

Jeannie looked puzzled.

'It's more of the rhyming slang,' Danny explained. 'Pony and trap. Rhymes with crap, so he is gone for a long slow you-know-what.'

Richie looked at Jeannie.

'So you thought it was good tonight?'

'It was really brilliant. I thought your hair looked amazing. Everybody's hair was amazing.' She looked back to Danny's hair and giggled.

'It's like a fucking Indian head-dress, isn't it?' he laughed. 'Anyway, what's the story? We're going to Lillie's Bordello, so if you want to come for a drink, speak up now, the coach leaves in two minutes flat.'

It was unusual for Danny to invite Jeannie along when the other members of the band were with him. Sean was the only one who knew what was between them. Jeannie didn't let surprise register on her face, but she caught Richie looking at her. She returned his glance and he looked away.

'OK, so who is coming with me?' Snake said as he walked in the door.

'I'll go with you,' Frankie answered. 'I think my girlfriend, Carol, is probably waiting outside for me as well.'

'I'll take Sean,' Danny volunteered. 'And of course the girls.'

'What about you, Richie?' Snake asked.

'I'll go with Danny,' Richie replied hurriedly.

'That's cool,' Danny said, exchanging glances with Jeannie.

Twelve

The manager was inside the door when Danny arrived at the club.

'I hear the gig was great. Snake has a table for you, down

67

at the back,' he said.

'Thanks,' Danny said over his shoulder, as he led his party of people down the stairs.

The powerful beat came thumping through the door. Inside, people stood squashed together as the huge Thursday night crowd enjoyed themselves. Danny nosed his way through them. Dancers stopped and looked at his make-up and his startling haircut and some moved out of his way, whispering behind their hands as he passed.

A stocky young man blocked Danny's path. His tie was pulled down inches from the neck of his shirt. He swayed belligerently in front of Danny, his eyes glazed from too much drink.

'You're that bollocks that attacked Bono and Bob Geldof, aren't you?' he spat accusingly.

Danny's eyes went cold and hard, but a smile stayed on his face.

'You got me in one.'

'Bob Geldof is a great person,' the drunk continued. 'You're not fit to lick his boots.'

'And you're not fit to lick my arse,' Danny snarled.

All around them in their immediate tight circle, people shifted uneasily. No one could hear above the loud music, but everyone could see there was trouble coming. Suddenly Danny moved, his knee crashing into the drunk's groin. A look of startled pain crossed the man's face, as he sank to his knees clutching himself.

The bouncers arrived seconds later. Danny quickly explained the situation. The manager ushered them to their table, instructing the bouncers to have the drunk ejected.

'Was he a music critic?' Sean laughed jovially, as they sat at the table.

Jeannie was conscious that everyone in their immediate area was looking at her table and whispering. She leaned close to Danny.

'Do you think I should leave? There's a lot of attention on you tonight.'

He squeezed her thigh underneath the table, shaking his head as he did so.

For the next hour, Jeannie was happy. She felt Danny's warm leg touching hers and she thought back to the touch of his fingers the night before. It gave her a little shiver to think about it and she wondered whether Danny would want to make love to her again tonight.

The waitress appeared at Danny's elbow. 'Excuse me, but there's a phone call for you in the office.' Danny looked at Jeannie, his eyes telling her that he didn't know who the caller might be. He excused himself and made his way downstairs.

'This way,' the manager said, leading him through to his office.

Danny lifted the phone. 'Who is this please?'

'Danny, it's me,' came Mary's voice.

'Is there a problem?' he asked.

'Deirdre has been very sick for the past two hours. I'm not trying to spoil your fun, but I would like to have the car here just in case she gets any worse.'

'Did you ring the doctor?'

'No, not yet. I'm not sure how bad she is,' Mary answered. 'But in case she gets any worse, I'd like to feel I could drive her around to Harcourt Street Hospital.'

'OK. I'll be right there.'

'Don't break your neck getting here.'

'Yeah. All right. See ya.' He put the phone down and mouthed a silent oath.

Danny walked back outside. He called the manager. 'Do me a favour. Would you tell Snake and the gang I had to leave. One of the kids is sick. If I go back in, I'll get stuck trying to explain to everyone.'

'Sure, sure. No problem.'

Danny crossed Grafton Street diagonally into Wicklow Street. As he passed by the bottom of Clarendon Street, three figures loomed out of the shadows. They dragged Danny in behind a van, out of sight of the street. Danny had time to recognise the stocky drunk before the first punch hit him in the eye. A kick into his groin followed. Danny felt an excruciating burst of pain and slid to the ground. A foot kicked him in the face. He heard a crack and he knew that his nose was broken. Blood began to spurt from his nose, as a rain of kicks landed on his shoulders, neck and head. Danny kept his hands over his head.

'You fucking bollocks. I'll fucking kill you.' Danny recognised the voice from his earlier fracas.

'Quick, lads! Someone's coming.'

The three men took off, running up Wicklow Street. A couple passed by but they were so engrossed in each other, they didn't see Danny. He dragged himself painfully to his feet. Holding the side of his hand under his nose, he tried to stem the flow of blood. He staggered back across the road. As he reached the door of the club two girls were coming out. They saw Danny's face and screamed. The doormen hurried Danny inside.

'Get Snake,' Danny whispered through his pain.

Snake and Sean both appeared in seconds. Jeannie, white-faced, stood behind them.

'Sweet Jaysus,' Sean exclaimed, when he saw the mess that Danny's face was in.

'Mother-fucker,' Snake said. 'We'd better get you to a hospital. Call an ambulance.'

'No ambulance,' Danny spat. 'No fucking ambulance.'

'All right,' Snake acquiesced. 'Sean, will you drive Danny to the hospital in his car?'

'Ring Mary,' Danny moaned. 'She needs the car now. One

of the kids is sick.'

'I'll do that,' Snake said. 'Sean you drive him to the hospital. I'll call Mary. You can get the car to her as soon as you get Danny to the hospital.'

Sean helped Danny to his feet. 'C'mon mate, we'll have to see if there's any bits worth saving.'

Everybody looked askance at Sean. 'Fuck off, lads. He knows I don't mean it,' Sean said.

As soon as they had left, Snake walked into the manager's office. He picked up the phone and dialled. 'Is that the news desk? I think you should get a photographer over to the Adelaide Emergency Room. Danny, the lead singer from Poison Pig, has just been beaten up by some angry punters.'

Snake repeated the call three more times, covering the four main Dublin papers. Only when he had taken care of business did Snake ring Mary Toner. 'Listen, don't get alarmed, but somebody just kicked the shit out of Danny,' Snake said.

'Is he badly hurt?' Mary asked anxiously.

'I think he'll be all right, but his face is a mess. He was saying one of the kids is sick.'

'Deirdre is puking a lot and I just wanted the car around, in case.'

'Well, Sean has taken Danny to the Adelaide and he's bringing the car to you as soon as possible.'

'Will you ring me when you see how Danny is?'

'Sure, sure. Goodbye.'

Snake hung up the phone and smiled broadly. 'This boy Danny is a real gem.'

Thirteen

Danny woke the following morning to the sensation of a finger tracing the stitches across his nose. He looked up and saw his five-year-old daughter, Deirdre, looking down at him.

'Oooh,' she said, her face all scrunched up as if she was feeling the pain herself. 'Is it sore?'

Danny reached his own hand to the stitches and his eyes smarted as he pressed the wound.

'It sure is, baby,' he told her. 'Give me a kiss and make it better.'

The small girl reached down and kissed Danny's stitches.

'Now it's better,' she cooed triumphantly.

'Thank you, miss,' Danny laughed, struggling to a sitting position. 'Will you tell Mammy I'm awake?'

Deirdre scampered off the bed and he heard her light footsteps descending the stairs. 'Not too fast!' he yelled.

The shock of the night before had now been replaced by anger in Danny. Mary came into the room.

'I know what that little fucker looks like,' Danny said. 'And I'll get the little creep if it's the last thing I do.'

'It might be the last thing you do,' Mary answered caustically.

'Whose side are you on?' Danny asked querulously.

'I'm sure you could have avoided the first incident in the club if you had wanted to.'

'So that's it,' Danny said bitterly. 'It's because I was in the club, isn't it?'

'But that's part of your work, isn't it?' Mary said acidly. 'You are always telling me that you have to keep the image going. Who am I to argue?'

'That's what I like about you, you're really sympathetic

when somebody is beaten up. In case you forgot, I was on my way home here, when I was jumped.'

'That's very noble of you.'

'You fuck off with yourself,' Danny retorted angrily. 'If anyone is indifferent around here, it's not me. I've been working like a dog, between rehearsals and everything else, and you couldn't give a shit whether I'm alive or dead, as long as you have the car to go home to your snobby mother.'

'So, going home to my snobby mother takes care of my social life and everything else, does it?' Mary exploded angrily. 'You don't bother to bring me anywhere. As long as there's someone to take care of the kids and wash your clothes and make your food, you can carry on being a rock star and the rest of us can go to hell.'

'That's a great idea,' Danny said, his voice icy-cold.

Mary stalked angrily from the room. 'You bastard,' she said grimly, tears springing to her eyes.

'For fuck's sake, that's all I needed,' Danny said out loud, as he listened to Mary's footsteps receding down the stairs. He heard her shout at the children. The sound of Deirdre's crying immediately afterwards made him angry, but he didn't make a move. A few minutes later he heard the door slam and the strangled screech of the Citroen being revved too hard as Mary drove away.

*   *   *

The doorbell woke Danny from a light sleep. He padded down the stairs and opened it to find Sean grinning on the doorstep.

'How'ya,' Danny said. 'Come in. I'm on my own.'

'Where's Mary?' Sean asked.

'Gone to her mother's,' Danny said bitterly.

'Bit of a row, was there?' Sean asked.

'The usual crap about how I'm always in nightclubs and she's at home here scraping shit off babies' nappies. I'm black and fucking blue and she chooses to see red.'

'Well, I see you haven't had your sparkling wit kicked out of you anyway,' Sean remarked.

'What about the papers. Did you see them?' Danny asked.

'Did I see them?' Sean guffawed. 'How the hell could I not see them, when our picture is all over the front pages.'

'Desperate crap,' Danny said.

'Was there any mention of Jeannie from Mary? She's very obvious in the photographs.'

'Not yet,' Danny answered. 'But I think it's brewing. I think that's partly what this argument is about.'

'And how are you going to explain her away?'

'I'll just tell Mary that she's the young one we picked up on the way back from Kerry. I did already mention her in an off-hand way, as a bit of cover.'

'But how will you explain her being at the hospital?'

'I'll say that she was at the gig with her friend and we bumped into them later and you were having a drink with them blah-blah when I came staggering back in.'

Sean looked at the expression on Danny's face.

'You want me to cover for you again, don't you?'

'If you don't mind.' Danny half-smiled. 'It's the least you could do for the victim of a "savage assault by unknown assailants", to quote the *Evening Press*.'

Sometimes Sean felt really aggrieved at the way Danny assumed he would provide alibis and excuses. It was an abuse of their friendship, but in the present circumstances he decided it would be easier to bite his lip one more time.

'I can't stay now,' Sean said, turning to leave. 'We hope we can get a basic rhythm track of "Designer Aid" down tonight.'

'That's great. When will you need the vocal, d'ye think?' Danny asked.

'Well, what do you think? Would you be up to it by tomorrow?'

'I think so. All I was afraid of was that my breathing would be fucked up, but it seems to be all right. I'm sure I should be able to do it, maybe tomorrow night.'

'I'll tell Snake and the lads,' Sean said smiling. 'Keep cool, and remember, wanking makes your eyes go black, so if you're at it, we'll all know.'

Danny laughed as Sean let himself out. From his reflection in the mirror, Danny could see that he looked funny, with two great black eyes, six stitches across his nose, a cut over his left eye and a long abrasion down his left cheek. His eyes were puffed and closed, and his whole face hurt when he cracked a smile.

Danny pulled out his matchbox and his small brass pipe from the pocket of his jacket. He took the small lump of hash from the matchbox and filled his pipe, savouring the blue-black smoke, holding it deep in his lungs for several seconds until he felt the strange mellowness that tiptoed in with the smoke and his mind began to drift.

Fourteen

Richie pulled the brush roughly through his hair, letting it spring back upright as the brush stroke curved down over his ears. He could see Jeannie in the mirror, reading the *Sunday World*. She looked grim, sunk into the corner of the couch, her feet tucked under her.

'Aren't you going to go out at all today?' Richie asked pleasantly.

Jeannie looked up from the newspaper. 'No.' Her voice was flat and emotionless.

'You're in a bit of a bad mood, are you?'

'Listen, Richie.' She whirled angrily on him. 'I don't have to be in a good mood all the time. Nobody is in a good mood all the time, and if I want to be in a bad mood, that's my business.'

Richie was taken aback by the hardness in her voice.

'Hold on, Jeannie, all I did was try to ask in a friendly way if you were all right. Sunday is your day off and I thought you might be going out.'

'I'm sorry, Richie, I don't really mean to take it out on you. It's just that I'm used to dealing with my bad moods on my own.'

'OK,' Richie said. 'I just want you to know that you've got a friend, and if you want to talk about things that bother you, whatever you say to me won't go beyond the two of us.'

Jeannie looked at Richie. She could see by his eyes that his concern was genuine. More than that, she felt that in an instant, given the slightest encouragement, Richie would take her in his arms and comfort her.

'I'm heading into the studio now. If you want to come in at about eight-thirty, we'll probably be going around to the Foggy Dew for a drink during our break.'

'Will Danny be there?' Jeannie asked, trying to sound casual.

'I don't think so,' Richie answered. 'He did his vocal last night, but apparently he is still very sore.'

'How did he sing if he was so sore?' Jeannie asked.

'Because he's very determined. I think the kicking he got only made him angrier. Luckily his nose was broken very cleanly, so it didn't block up his breathing. But you'd want to have seen the cut of him. He looked like a boxer who had just got the crap beaten out of himself and his eyes were all closed up and puffed.'

Jeannie ached to see Danny. She wanted to brush his lips

with her finger. She wanted to cradle his head in her arms and talk softly to him. She wanted to see the wrinkles of his smile and feel his hot breath gently blowing on her neck. Fiercely she conjured up an image of Danny's face, but it dissolved into the bruised and bloody mess that she had wrapped in her arms three nights before.

'I'll see about coming in later,' Jeannie said. 'Thanks for the offer. I might come and I mightn't. It depends on how I feel.'

Richie picked up his leather jacket and slid it over his shoulders.

'You'll be welcome anyway,' he said.

He closed the door behind him and Jeannie felt tears trickling slowly down her cheeks. She wanted Danny. She needed him right now. She picked up the newspaper and looked again at the photograph. Danny's battered face stared out at her, blood dripping from the ugly gash across the bridge of his nose. More blood trickled down his nostrils, some of it congealed in an ugly black ridge that disappeared into his mouth. Another cut above his left eye had also started a small stream of blood. Just over his right shoulder Jeannie could see her own scared white face blinking in the harsh glare of the flash bulb. Sean was reaching out over Danny's left shoulder, trying to get his hand in front of the lens, to block the photographer.

It was a dramatic photograph. All of the daily papers and the evening papers had carried the pictures on Friday. It was obvious someone had tipped off the newspapers, as a photographer had been waiting when Sean had driven up. The flash bulb had taken Danny, Sean and Jeannie by total surprise. 'Fuck off, you scumbag,' Sean roared at the photographer.

When Snake arrived minutes later, he convinced Sean and Danny that the photographers from the other newspapers should be allowed get photographs as well. 'You have to show the bastards up for the small-minded fuckers they are,' reasoned Snake, hiding his glee at the success of his phone calls. One newspaper would have been enough. This was a bonus.

Danny had had his wound cleaned and stitched, then the hospital decided to send him home. Jeannie wanted to kiss him, but she had curbed her impulse and instead put her hand on his arm.

'Will you be all right?'

'I'll be fine. Thanks for coming to the hospital.'

Now as she looked again at the photograph, it all came flooding back to her, filling her with tenderness for Danny.

* * *

'Will they ever get tired of running that fucking photograph?' Danny grimaced at the huge picture on the front of the *Sunday World*. Mary had just brought him in a pot of tea. Mary looked and saw it was the same photograph of Danny, Sean and the girl with the small white face, the same girl who had been on the front page of the papers two days before.

'Who is that girl anyway?'

This was the moment Danny had been anxiously anticipating. He tried to keep his voice light and normal as he answered.

'That's the young girl myself and Sean gave the lift to on the way back from Kerry.'

'And what was she doing at the hospital?'

Danny was glad he had rehearsed the scenario with Sean.

'Herself and her friend were at the gig in the Baggot and we bumped into them later. Sean was having a drink with them when I staggered back in and I think everybody just panicked.'

'Enough to bring a young girl to the hospital with you?'

'What the fuck do I know?' Danny said. 'I didn't know

what was going on at that stage.'

Mary continued to look at him suspiciously, but Danny didn't flinch. At least he was telling the truth when he said that he hadn't known what was going on. It had been a big surprise to him to find Jeannie at the hospital.

'What's her name?' Mary asked.

'Jeannie,' Danny tried to sound casual. 'Jeannie Callanan.'

'Does she go to all your gigs?' Mary asked sarcastically.

'Oh for fuck's sake, are we going to go through all this again?'

'Yes,' Mary retorted angrily. 'I'm stuck here at home with two kids and you have little floosies chasing you around your gigs.'

Danny jumped from the bed, wincing with pain as his feet hit the floor. He had to go onto the attack. If he sat there Mary would continue to prod at him with questions. 'Is it time for you to fuck off to your mother's again? Or will I go, seeing as I'm the one who is always causing the trouble.'

'You're a bastard.' Mary looked at him evenly. 'Well you're not going to make me cry this time, Mister. I don't care where you go, or what you do.'

Danny pulled on his pants. 'A pity you didn't think of that before you started all this shouting.'

'Get out of here,' Mary screamed, 'before you wind up with more bruises.'

Danny slipped on his shoes as quickly as he could. He grabbed the sun-glasses and the baseball cap from the dressing-table and checked his jacket to make sure he had his matchbox and his pipe. Mary glared at him and stomped from the room. He waited until he heard her footsteps entering the sitting-room.

He hurried down the stairs, pulled the front door open and took a quick look up and down the street. There were hardly any people there. Danny pulled the door closed silently behind him and walked quickly to the corner. He looked back over his shoulder, breathed a sigh of relief and began walking towards St Stephen's Green.

Fifteen

The studio control-room was bathed in soft light. The harsh overhead lights had been turned off to create a mellow mood. For once, the mellowness was not intended to make anyone relax. The softness of the ambient light gave more emphasis to the small red, orange and green lights that belonged to the faders on each of the twenty-four channels on the sound desk. Above each channel, a small windowed meter registered the levels of each recorded track. Sean sat staring at the meter, which was measuring the sound level of the rhythm guitar track.

'There's somethin' weird about Track 9,' he said, turning to the sound engineer.

'What do you mean?'

'The level just seems to be dropping slightly on the guitar break.'

'We'll have a look at it this time,' said the engineer.

'OK. Let her rip.'

The sound of the count-in clicked through the speakers as the engineer pressed the PLAY button, triggering the twenty-four track recording machine, which stood behind the desk.

'One, two, three, four ... Kerchaannng.' The first chord of 'Designer Aid' boomed out through the speakers. The two men listened intently, watching the meters. Behind them, sitting along the banquette seating, Frankie and Richie sat engrossed in magazines.

In the corner, Snake sneaked a glance at his watch. It said

4.30pm. No one else would be allowed to look at a watch or clock. 'Concentration on the track,' Snake urged. 'I want it to be right, so take as long as is necessary.'

Now they were on their third day. Snake had been tempted to cancel the session when Danny had been beaten up, but Sean had convinced him to go ahead. Sean had the most experience of recording, and Danny and Sean had convinced Snake that Sean should produce the single, instead of calling in outside help. 'We know what we're looking for,' Danny had counselled. 'If you bring in some wanker from outside, he'll start fuckin' around with *our* sound and it could take forever.'

'Trust us,' Sean said.

Snake had trusted them, and Sean had somehow cajoled Danny into giving a brilliant vocal performance, despite feeling so sore. As he listened to the playback, Snake felt excited. The song sounded like a real hit single. Danny's wounded, angry voice conveyed the sarcastic message of the song.

'Can you give me a bit more reverb on the snare?' Sean asked.

The engineer reached across and twiddled one of the blue knobs on channel 3. The sound of the snare drum went a few feet further out into space, the sound getting a bit more hollow.

'That's the business,' Sean said.

The playback finished. Sean swivelled in his chair and looked at Snake, Richie and Frankie. 'What d'ye think?'

'It sounds great,' Richie said.

'What do you think, Frankie?'

'Sounds cool to me, but I think that the sound on my guitar track ...'

'Hold it, hold it,' Sean interrupted. 'We haven't fiddled with the sounds yet at all. That's just our recording playback. We're going into the mix mode now.'

'How long will it take to mix?' Snake asked.

'How long is a piece of string?' Sean grinned.

The engineer chipped in. 'It'll take me a while to set up the mix mode.'

'The drum sound will probably take about an hour, hour and a half,' Sean said knowledgeably, 'and the rest of the sounds will come as we're going along. I'd say about six to eight hours. I think the best thing now is that we set up for the mix, get a drum sound and then myself and "Mr Knobs" here will take a break for some grub.'

'Well, it's six-thirty now, so what time do you think you'll start mixing?' Snake asked.

'About eight-thirty or so.'

'Do I have to be here at eight-thirty?' Richie enquired.

'Well, it's not essential, Richie, but if you want to be here that's fine.'

'I do,' Richie said. 'It's just that I have a kind of half arrangement to see someone in the pub at eight-thirty.'

'Whooo!' Sean jeered. 'Richie has a heavy date.'

'Actually, it's just Jeannie,' Richie said, throwing it out as lightly as he could. 'She was a bit mopey today when I was leaving the flat, so I told her if she wanted to come in at the break, she could have a drink with us. But at that stage I thought we'd be breaking at about eight.'

'Well, don't panic, Richie, we won't do a mix without you. And if she promises to shut up, you can bring Jeannie over for a while if you like. Just don't let Broken Nose catch you.'

Richie beamed his thanks to Sean. He would get a chance to have a drink with Jeannie and also show her how the studio worked. Danny was safely home in bed. Tonight he would have Jeannie to himself.

Sixteen

Jeannie watched the hands on the clock inch their way towards eight o'clock. She had been staring at the clock for at least ten minutes, her mind filled with thoughts of Danny. He hadn't been in touch with her since Friday. She had grown used to the daily contact, and even two days without seeing him had already caused her to fret. Now a third day was almost over and Jeannie felt as though her head was going to burst.

The phone rang in the hall. Jeannie waited to see if any of the other tenants in the house would answer and then she opened the door and stepped to the phone.

'Hello?'

'Hello. I'd like to speak to Jeannie Callanan please.'

Jeannie recognised her mother's voice immediately. She went instantly cold and a wave of panic engulfed her. What could she tell her mother about the photographs? How could she explain all this mess?

Since she had run away from home, Jeannie had written to her mother every week. Her letters were short, friendly and optimistic, but economical with the truth. She said she was sharing a flat with another girl and she gave the phone number, but asked her mother not to contact her except in an emergency. She said she was working in a restaurant. But she didn't mention Danny or the band. By keeping the tone of her letters bright and breezy, she hoped to allay her mother's fears about her well-being, but she knew her mother would be distraught with worry about the photographs.

She stared at the phone. Then she splayed her fingers over the mouthpiece and assumed a strong Dublin accent.

'Hold on and I'll see if she's in her flat,' she said shakily.

Jeannie let the phone drop and hang by its cord. She went

through the charade of walking to her door and knocking on it. She waited and then returned to the phone.

'There's no answer. She mustn't be in.'

'OK,' her mother said hesitantly. 'Excuse me, but could you leave a message for her?'

'Yeah,' Jeannie grunted.

She noticed the anxiety in her mother's voice, but when she had finished, Jeannie simply said a quick goodbye and hung the phone back on its cradle. She let a breath whistle through her lips and lay against the wall. What should she do? Should she ring her mother before her father decided to take some action? What could he do? Did he care one way or another? Was she putting her mother through hell?

'Oh Danny,' she groaned. If only Danny were around, he would know what to do. Why hadn't he called her? Would she dare phone him? Did her parents know about her involvement with Danny? Was it obvious from the photographs?

Jeannie walked wearily back into the flat. She crossed to her small bedroom and bent down to look at herself in the mirror of the dressing-table. 'Jesus, I look desperate,' she said to her reflection.

She dabbed at her face with her hand and then, making an instant decision, she decided to go without make-up, except for lipstick, which she applied carefully. She tousled her hair, frowned disgustedly and, taking a small woollen cap from a drawer, pulled it on, fixing it in place with two hair-clips. 'I'll have to do,' she said, once more addressing her reflection.

She picked up a small handbag, took her heavy cardigan from the hook on the back of the bedroom door and walked through the sitting-room, turning off the table lamp as she went.

Jeannie hurried to the bus stop. Richie had said they would be taking a break at eight-thirty. Oh Danny, why couldn't Danny be there!

* * *

The heavy thump of a bass drum was the only sound in the control-room. Sean sat at the desk listening to the booming sound, cocking his ears and looking from speaker to speaker as though he could see the sound.

'A little more delay on the bass drum, if possible,' Sean requested.

'Your funeral,' came the terse reply.

'Listen, Knobs, I know everybody doesn't put delay on the bass drum, but I think it helps our sound, so let's try it.'

The buzzer on the door intercom rang. Sean sprang from his chair, picking up the receiver from its cradle.

'Dundrum Mental Hospital, can I help?' he cackled into the mouthpiece.

'This is oul' Broken Nose. I've reserved the Rubber Room for two nights,' came Danny's voice through the crackly speaker.

'Jaysus, we thought you were dead,' Sean laughed.

They waited in silence for Danny to ascend the two flights of stairs. They saw him appear around the edge of the studio door. He walked towards them, framed in half-light in the big picture window of the control-room.

Danny pulled open the control-room door and stepped inside, falling a little to his right and bumping the wall.

'The oul' pins not too steady yet?' Sean queried, eyebrows raised.

'Definitely four faults all right,' Danny said thickly, a big silly grin spreading over his face.

'Jaysus, you're a desperate man, Danny,' Sean said. 'You're arseholes drunk.'

'It's not me. It's women. They're all bastards.'

'Did you eat anything? Or where the fuck were you? Or what are you at?'

'I was in Bruxelles, Peter's Pub, the Bailey, Davy Byrne's, Neary's, the International Bar and I am on my way to yet another pub.'

Sean suddenly remembered that Richie was meeting Jeannie in the local pub. Despite his amiable tone, Sean knew that Danny was in one of his wicked drunken moods. In his current state, Danny would be in danger of stirring up a lot of trouble. He certainly wouldn't be too pleased to see Richie with Jeannie.

'I presume you can't go home right now?' Sean asked.

'You're a great presumer,' Danny replied, punching Sean on the upper arm.

'Why don't you get a taxi to my place?' Sean suggested. 'And you can have a kip and come back in for the end of the mix.'

'Because I don't want to go to your place. And I don't want to have a kip. I want to go to the pub. And I don't give a fuck about the mix.'

Before he could say any more, the engineer returned with three cups of coffee.

'Get that into you,' Sean said, handing Danny a cup of black coffee. 'Me and Knobs here are going for a pizza, so you might as well come along and get a bit of ballast in, if you're going to keep on drinking.'

Danny looked at Sean balefully. 'You're a terrible sensible bastard all the same.'

Danny drank the black coffee slowly, while Sean and the engineer worked at the drum sound. When they were happy with the sound, they put on their jackets, got Danny to his feet and pushed him protestingly down the stairs and out into the street.

'Where are we going?' Danny bellowed.

'We're going around the corner for a pizza,' Sean told him. Danny's eyes lit up. Jeannie worked in the pizza restaurant.

'Maybe Jeannie is working,' Danny said.

'I don't think so,' Sean said anxiously, trying to steer Danny's thoughts away from Jeannie.

It was an uneasy meal for Sean. Danny was constantly just one step away from truculence. 'I'll tell you somethin', Sean,' he said loudly, 'this fucking business is full of shitheads.' His words rang out through the restaurant, which was quiet and not very busy.

'Keep your voice down,' Sean hissed. 'You're not exactly in the privacy of your own home.'

'Listen, Sean, don't keep fucking telling me what to do. I'm not a bleedin' child y'know, so fuck off.'

Sean looked at the engineer and then back at Danny. 'I think it's time to go back to the studio.'

'You can go,' Danny said, in a big loud voice. 'I'm staying to finish my glass of wine.'

'Danny,' Sean spoke quietly through his teeth. 'You're being a terrible pain in the arse. Now c'mon back to the studio.'

Danny gave Sean a cold hard grin. 'You're a very nice fella, Sean, but you're a terrible fuckin' worrier.'

'Aw, fuck you.'

Sean turned angrily and stormed to the cashier's desk. He paid the bill and left, the engineer following close behind.

Danny sat alone in the midst of four empty tables. The other customers had turned to look in his direction. He sat there looking bizarre in his baseball cap, dark glasses, black jacket and black dungarees. He called a waitress.

'Where's Jeannie? Is she not working today?'

'No,' the waitress answered, keeping her distance. 'I don't think she's in until tomorrow.'

'Yeah, yeah,' Danny said rudely, not bothering to thank her. 'Fuck you, Jeannie,' he muttered to himself. 'Why aren't you here?'

Seventeen

On the way back to the studio, Sean took a quick detour. He pushed open the door of the pub. A sing-song was going on in the corner. Sean walked in and saw Richie and Jeannie sitting at a back table, talking quietly.

Richie looked up as Sean approached.

'How'ya,' Sean said. 'I just came to warn you that Danny is up the street, pissed out of his brain and he's on his way here.'

'Danny!' the word slipped out of Jeannie's mouth.

'You only know Danny as a happy drunk, Jeannie,' Sean said. 'But he has a wicked side too and my own advice is that the two of you get the fuck out of here before he gets here.'

'Too late,' Richie cursed, as he spotted Danny coming round the door.

Danny stood and swayed on his feet. He looked around the pub. He caught sight of Sean and his gaze travelled on down to Richie and Jeannie.

Sean made one last attempt to control Danny.

'Are you coming back to help with the mix, Danny?' he asked, barring Danny's way to Richie's table.

'Am I, fuck!' Danny said. 'I'm going to stay here and have a drink with my friends Richie and Jeannie, amn't I?'

Danny pushed past Sean and pulled out a stool and sat opposite Richie and Jeannie. His face screwed up into an evil leer.

'So this is romance, Dublin style,' Danny spat.

'Hello, Danny,' Jeannie said quietly. 'How are you feeling?'

'Is this a medical or a personal enquiry?' Danny asked sarcastically.

'I'm asking as a friend,' Jeannie said, the hurt in her eyes visible to Richie.

'Danny, I think you're a bit over the top,' Richie said.

'Is that fucking so, Richie my boy? Would you be an expert on over-the-topness or something? I was just asking my good friend Jeannie here a question.'

'And she was trying to be nice to you,' Richie said tersely.

'You're right,' Danny said, appearing to soften. 'I'm sorry, Jeannie. Forgive me for being rude.' Danny beamed one of his big winning smiles. Richie felt a mixture of anger and resentment welling up inside, but he forced himself to smile back at Danny.

'What'll you have to drink?' Richie asked.

'I'd like a vodka and tonic – and I'll leave the size to yourself.'

Richie got up from the table and walked to the bar. Danny looked across at Jeannie, his eyes growing hard again. 'You don't wait long, do you?'

'What do you mean?'

'I mean, I don't see you for two days because I'm in fucking bed and here you are out on the town.'

'Hold on, Danny. I'm not out on the town. Richie just asked me, out of the goodness of his heart, if I wanted to come in and join everybody for a drink, while they were having a break. I thought Frankie and Sean and Snake would be here as well.'

'Well, it's a good job they aren't, isn't it,' Danny said venomously. 'If they were, you wouldn't be able to have this little romantic twosome with Richie.'

'Danny, please stop,' she begged. 'I've spent the last three days moping around because I couldn't see you and I just didn't want to be on my own again tonight. Please understand.'

'I understand,' Danny said loudly, as Richie returned with drinks for the three of them.

The barman leaned across the counter.

'Keep the noise down over there,' he said, glaring across at Danny.

'Yeah, yeah.' Danny acknowledged him with a wave of his forefinger. He turned back to Richie.

'So how's it goin', Richie? Are you going to help with the mix or are you too busy on the social circuit to have any words of wisdom for Poison Pig?'

'As it happens,' Richie said, 'I was going to go back in a while and I was going to bring Jeannie in and let her see what goes on at a mix.'

'Fuck me, educational as well as romantic,' Danny sneered.

Richie felt his temper rising. He leaned across to Danny, and spoke softly and menacingly. 'Danny, I know that you already got the shit kicked out of you once this week, but if you don't want it to happen again, you'd better shut up right now.'

'For fuck's sake, Barry McGuigan on bass.'

Richie sprang at Danny across the table. The sudden assault knocked Danny backwards. His drink flew out of his hand as he knocked over a table.

The barman jumped over the counter and dragged Richie off Danny.

'I'll kill the bastard,' Richie shrieked.

Jeannie stood horrified and confused. She wanted to bend down to Danny, who was still on the floor, but she didn't want to anger Richie any further. He was fighting on her behalf.

'You're out, Danny,' the barman said.

'You know me?' Danny said, in a surprised tone.

'Yeah, I know you. And if you keep going the way you are, you'll have a permanent black eye.'

The barman pulled Danny by his two arms towards the door. Danny turned his head.

'OK, OK, I'm going. Don't forget to give him a good ride,' he shouted, looking straight into Jeannie's eyes.

Jeannie burst into tears. Richie made a move to jump for Danny again, but the barman dragged him quickly to the door, pulled it open and pushed him out into the street. 'If I were you, pal, I'd fuck off now before I get in any more trouble.'

*   *   *

Richie checked the street carefully for signs of Danny. Then he walked to the corner and looked up and down, before going back to the pub door where Jeannie stood waiting.

'It's all right, he's gone. I'll get you a taxi now.'

They rode in the taxi in silence, Richie putting his arm around Jeannie whose tear-stained face rested on his shoulder. Jeannie felt numb. How could Danny be so cruel! How could this man that she loved suddenly become so cold and insulting!

Richie paid the taxi-driver and they went into the flat.

'Can I make you a cup of coffee or anything?' he asked.

'I'd like a cup of coffee,' Jeannie answered, looking at Richie.

She sat on the couch and Richie came with two cups of coffee and sat beside her. He reached out and wiped a small tear-stain from her cheek. She looked at his soft gentle eyes, and then Richie was kissing her, his moist lips pressing on Jeannie's. Jeannie didn't pull back. She let Richie kiss her, pushing his tongue softly into her mouth. Why couldn't it be Danny, she thought, closing her eyes. Then a sudden hardness took over her thoughts. Danny is not here and Richie is. She allowed Richie's arm to enfold her and she began kissing him back.

Richie's kisses were growing in ardour. He started to push Jeannie down onto the couch, moving his body so that he could let her lie out flat. She felt the full length of his body along hers.

'No, Richie, please stop,' she panted. 'Not tonight.'

Richie pulled himself up on one elbow. 'What's the matter?'

'I just can't, right now.'

She saw the disappointment in Richie's eyes.

'There'll be other times,' she said.

Richie watched Jeannie as she rose and walked to the bedroom door. He had kissed her and she had kissed him back. She turned at the door and looked at him.

'Good night. And thanks again.'

'You're welcome,' he smiled.

Eighteen

Snake used all of his charm to preserve peace in Poison Pig. The coolness between Danny and Richie had been having its effect in more ways than one. Danny had been at home all the time, which meant that Mary was off-limits. Snake had not been too pleased about having to forego his physical pleasure.

Despite the rift in the band, Snake was feeling mighty smug. Three out of four Sunday papers had carried further details of the assault on Danny. The photograph on the front page of the *Sunday World* had been worth thousands of pounds in advertising.

Monday morning had brought them a page three story in a British tabloid. 'GELDOF BASHER GETS BASHED' read the headline that accompanied the photograph of the bruised Danny. The story got five paragraphs, calling Poison Pig 'Ireland's most controversial band'.

Mary answered the phone when Snake rang to talk to Danny.

'Hi, Mary. I wish I was there with you, body to body and I know you can't say anything and I'm just teasing and I'll talk to you later.'

'Bastard,' Mary whispered into the phone. Then she let her voice rise to normal level. 'It's for you, Danny, it's Snake,' she called.

Danny took the phone.

'What's the story?'

'The story is that there is an awful lot of activity. I got two phone calls from London, I have half of Ireland looking for dates, I have more publicity than I ever hoped for and I have the lead singer of the band having a war with the bass player.'

'Look,' Danny said forcefully. 'It's not war. It's no big deal. I've just been a bit grumpy for the last few days, but it'll be all right.'

'Well, that's good news. Have you spoken to Richie at all?'

'No, not yet. But I will before Thursday.'

'Don't bother,' Snake said. 'I'm calling a band meeting for Thursday afternoon and I'll tell Richie to come at two o'clock and everybody else to come at a quarter past two. If you're here at two, you and Richie can talk it out.'

'That's what I love about you, Snake. If it can't be talked out in fifteen minutes ... Jaysus, if only life was that easy.'

'It is,' Snake said. 'It's only a minor row over a bit of crumpet.'

Danny bristled. Since the fight on Sunday night he had thought of Jeannie every minute of the day. He could not get the image of Jeannie and Richie together out of his brain. At night, as he lay in bed, he had tormented himself that Richie was lying in bed with Jeannie, making slow, languorous love to her.

'Yeah, you're right,' Danny said, biting his lip, determined not to let Snake hear the pain in his voice.

* * *

Jeannie walked to a pick-up counter of the café. She was carrying a pepperoni pizza.

'Steve?'

The chef looked at Jeannie.

'Is there a complaint?' he asked

'No,' Jeannie said embarrassedly, 'I took the wrong order.'

The chef looked at her, his face sympathetic rather than angry.

'That's three mistakes in a row, Jeannie. Is something bothering you?'

Jeannie got flustered. She didn't know what to say. She felt her face flush bright red.

'I got a bit of bad news from home,' she stammered.

'OK, OK.' The chef looked concerned. 'What do you want instead of this?'

'Sausage and peppers, please.'

Tears sprang to Jeannie's eyes once more. Every day since the fight between Danny and Richie, she had surrendered to uncontrollable fits of crying.

Richie had pretended not to notice the tears. He sat with her and listened to tapes, talking to her and trying to be with her without putting any pressure on.

A lot of the time, Jeannie didn't appear to be listening, either to the tapes or to the words that Richie was saying. Richie took Jeannie to the zoo. It was a crisp, cold day and they enjoyed walking in the brittle sunshine. They stopped at the chimpanzees' enclosure and likened the chimps to various members of the band, stopping short of mentioning Danny. As they walked around the zoo, Richie slid his hand into Jeannie's. She didn't object. Richie was elated, and they laughed and strolled hand in hand.

'Richie, I just want to say thanks for today. And the last few days. You've been a really good friend to me.'

'It was nothing.' Richie shrugged. 'That's what friends are for.'

He looked at her, reaching out with his hand to touch her face.

'Would you mind if I kissed you?' he asked her.

Jeannie looked back at him, at his gentle mouth, his gentle eyes and his puppy-dog expression, wishing that it was Richie she loved instead of Danny.

'Just let's not get carried away,' she smiled, as his lips closed on hers.

Nineteen

'Everybody is talking about you,' Sean said to Danny. 'Even those who don't agree with you are still upset that you got kicked around for what you said.'

'Because they all know there's a grain of truth in it,' Danny said. 'Anyway, it's not so much what I believe in, as the stroke we have going here. I really don't give a fuck what Bono or Sting or anybody else does.'

Sean didn't make any comment.

'Well y'know what I mean,' Danny said. 'I mean it's a gig and we're doing the gig? Right?'

Sean looked hard at Danny before he spoke. 'This time a couple of months ago we were both broke, playing poxy gigs and we had nothin' going for us. Now we have a gig and a possible deal. It's better than fuck-all. Better than being the smallest Caribbean band in the world,' he laughed.

Danny didn't smile.

'Yeah, but how do you really *feel* about it?'

'I'm a bit like you, Danny. I don't really give a monkey's

piss what Bono or Sting or Geldof or anybody thinks really, but I think they are a bit posey so it doesn't bother me to go on slaggin' them.'

'Yeah,' Danny said pensively. 'It's just sometimes I think, shite, we're not really doing our own music even though we're writing the songs. It's all a con.'

'So where does that leave Snake?' Sean asked.

'Fucking right,' Danny answered. 'Now there's a slithery fuck if ever there was one. Maybe we are doing a service to our brother musicians by taking the greasy rat's money.'

'Oooh, the boy is recovering,' Sean smiled.

Danny looked at Sean. 'Have you seen Jeannie at all?'

'Well, I wouldn't be in the way of seein' her.'

'What about Richie? Have you seen him?' Danny asked.

'Yeah, I was talking to Richie earlier today. The single was cut this morning,' Sean replied.

'Yeah, I know. Snake told me. What did Richie say?'

'Not a lot, really. I think he thinks the whole thing has been blown out of proportion and I don't think there'll be any further hassle.'

'Sean, look at me and tell me straight. D'you think there's a scene going on between Richie and Jeannie?'

Sean read the real concern in Danny's eyes. 'Not that I know of. If you want my honest opinion, I think she's in love with you. But where the fuck do you go from here?'

'I know, I know. My head is in a bit of a spin over her. What the fuck can I do?'

Sean looked at him levelly. 'You're not expecting me to give you advice are you? 'Cos you'll ignore it anyway.'

Danny smiled. 'You're right. What's the story on turf?'

'I have a bit,' Sean answered. 'Are you very low?'

'I've enough to get me through tonight,' Danny said, 'as long as it's only twelve, never-ending, poxy hours long.'

'That's pretty long all right.'

Twenty

Mary dropped her money into the slot of the coin-box and phoned Snake's office. Snake answered the phone. 'Endless Talent Limited.'

'Snake, it's Mary. Can you talk?'

'Yeah, I'm on my own.'

'Do you want to meet me tonight?' Mary asked.

'How come?'

'Danny is hell-bent on staying home and I had arranged to go out with a friend of mine, Maura Doherty, so I'm going to get Danny to drive me and I'll tell him that Maura will give me a lift home.'

'Where will I see you?'

'I'll see you outside the Old Stand. It should be about ten past eleven. Maura has to be home early, so it won't be any bother to get away.'

'The pubs will be closed,' he cautioned. 'So where will we go?'

There was a moment's hesitation.

'Could we buy a bottle and go back to your place?' Mary ventured.

'I'm sure we could. And if we want to go out later, we could always go to Leeson Street.'

'Would that be safe?' Mary asked.

'Yeah. We'll just go to a club that none of our lads would go to.'

So what if Danny spotted them, Mary thought. He was out every night in clubs. It might snap him to his senses. But did she want Danny to come to his senses? The sex with Snake was rough and exciting and he always had coke or speed. When she was stoned her guilt became manageable, but now she was sober and straight and the thought of the terrible

97

consequences to her relationship with Danny and what would happen to the band if her affair with Snake became public knowledge gave her a moment's pause.

'Can we decide on that later?' Mary asked.

'Sure, babe,' Snake replied. 'Anyway, you'll be too exhausted to go to a club by the time I'm finished with you,' he laughed.

*   *   *

Richie looked at the television listlessly, knowing that he was not ready to sleep. He searched his pocket for coins and walked out to the public telephone in the hallway. He rang Sean's number.

'Hello, is Sean home?'

'Hang on.'

'Hello?' Sean said.

'Sean, it's Richie.'

'Richie. How's it going?'

'Good, good. I was just wondering, are you going for a drink, or are you going to bed or what?'

'I wish I *was* going for a what,' Sean laughed. 'What had you got in mind?'

'I just thought we might go down to Lillie's for a few drinks,' Richie said.

'Did you win the lottery or somethin'?'

'You'd never know,' Richie chuckled. 'So what do you think?'

'It's cool by me,' Sean said.

'OK. See you in about half an hour?'

'Right.'

*   *   *

Snake pulled the car into the kerb just over Leeson Street Bridge. He was feeling very happy with himself. He and Mary had driven to his flat and consumed a bottle of vodka between them. Before they left Snake's flat, they had snorted two lines of coke. 'A special treat for a special lady,' Snake had smiled. Now as they sat in the car, they both felt well in control again.

'That was nice coke,' Snake said. 'Really straightens you out after the booze.'

'Mmm.' Mary looked at Snake. 'How come the big splurge on coke?'

'Well, after all the publicity we got over the weekend, I thought I'd give myself a little treat. If we'd had to pay for all those photographs, it would have cost about twenty grand.'

Mary's eyes narrowed as Snake mentioned the photographs.

'Who is this girl Jeannie in the photographs?' Mary asked.

Snake's alarm system began to jangle. How much did Mary know? Should he tell her that he thought Danny and Jeannie were having an affair?

He tried to sound as off-hand as possible.

'She's just a kid who comes to see the band. I think Danny and Sean gave her a lift up from Kerry or something like that.'

'And how come she was in the photographs?' Mary asked.

'We bumped into her at the club,' he lied. 'To be quite honest with you, there was so much confusion that I didn't know anybody had gone to the hospital with Sean and Danny.'

Mary looked at him, trying to read his eyes. Snake met her gaze levelly.

'Are you ready?'

She nodded.

'OK, here we go.'

*　　*　　*

Sean and Richie stood close to the bar. Even though it was Tuesday, the place was packed. Shane Leahy, a song-writer, joined them and the banter was bright and lively, but the big crowd was freaking Richie. He couldn't handle the claustrophobic loudness of it all. He tugged at Sean's sleeve.

'Are you planning to go anywhere else?' Richie asked.

Sean immediately saw the distress in Richie's eyes, but he didn't pretend.

'Sure thing, me oul' scout. Where would you like to go?'

'I don't know,' Richie replied. 'Are the lads going anywhere?'

Sean turned to the song-writer.

'Are you guys going anywhere?' Sean asked.

'We'll probably go to Suesey Street in a few minutes,' came the reply.

'Will you give us a lift?'

'No problem.'

'Do we have to go to Suesey's?' Sean asked.

'Have you any better idea?'

'It's just that we always go to Suesey's and Richie here is on a night of adventure, so we might as well entertain him by going somewhere we don't normally go,' Sean explained.

'There's nothing like a bit of social intrepidity.'

They parked the car at the top of Pembroke Street and giggled their way as far as the nightclub.

'Good evening. In good form, are we?' the doorman quipped.

'Great form,' Sean laughed. 'Not pissed, just great form.'

Inside it was quiet enough. Three couples were dancing, and about ten other people were dotted around the bar. Down along the back of the club, several more couples sat at tables.

'Where's the john?' Richie asked. 'I'm bursting.'

'I'm not sure,' Sean said.

Richie walked down past the bar. Beyond the corridor of tables he lifted his eyes from the floor just in time to see Snake planting a passionate kiss on Mary's lips.

'Oh Jesus,' Richie whispered to himself, and turned on his heel and scurried back to Sean.

'We've got to get out of here, Sean,' he hissed.

'What's the matter with you now?' Sean said, a hint of impatience creeping into his voice.

Richie grabbed Sean's arm and dragged him to the end of the bar. Tucking himself in behind two drinkers so that they wouldn't be spotted, he pointed to Snake and Mary.

'Suffering Jaysus!' Sean exclaimed. 'You're right, Richie. Let's get the hell out of here.'

Sean and Richie rejoined their companion.

'Richie is feeling sick, so we're going outside for some air. If we don't come back, we'll see you round. OK?'

'You're great company,' laughed the song-writer sarcastically. 'Remind me to go out with you guys more often.'

Sean and Richie bounded up the steps to the street. They looked at one another.

'Keep your beak shut,' Sean said, 'no matter what else you do.'

'Don't worry, I won't say a word to anyone.'

Sean hailed a taxi. Himself and Richie sat in silence as the car nosed its way up St Stephen's Green.

Fuck you, Mary, Sean thought to himself. And fuck you too, Danny. And fuck you, Snake. His best friends were now in a complete muddle of intrigue, and Snake, whom Danny despised, had proven to be even sneakier than any of them had suspected. Danny would surely get physical with him and after that what would happen to the band? And what would happen to Danny and Mary? And Danny and Jeannie?

Anger began to rise inside him. He was stuck in the middle, lying to Mary about Danny and lying to Jeannie about Mary and now he was stuck with the dilemma of whether to tell Danny about Snake and Mary.

'Stop the car, please,' Sean said. The cab pulled over to the kerb. 'Have you enough money, Richie?' Sean opened the door.

'Yeah,' Richie replied. 'But where are you off to?'

'I just want to walk. I need time to think. See you tomorrow.'

The cab pulled away into traffic. Sean took a run at a Coke can that was lying against the kerb and kicked it viciously into the air. The rattle and clang as it landed in a basement yard echoed in the empty street, with a sound as hollow as the feeling in the pit of his stomach.

Twenty-one

Danny and Sean climbed from Danny's car and began walking the short distance from the visitors' car park to the main television studio block. Danny was in a rage. He had driven to the barrier at the security hut on the driveway and explained that he and Sean were to appear on the 'Late Late Show'. His explanation had met with stony indifference.

'I'm sorry, sir, only cars with a staff pass are allowed past this point.'

As they came abreast of the security hut, Danny threw an imaginary hand-grenade in its direction.

'Two-bit jumped-up bastards in uniforms,' he spat.

Danny threw a sidelong glance and caught Sean sniggering at his outrage.

'Sorry,' Danny laughed. 'I was busy being a big rock star.' He pushed through the revolving door of the studios, Sean at his heels. Inside in the lobby, Snake was anxiously looking at his watch. He smiled as he saw them come towards him.

'I was getting a bit worried in case you chickened out,' Snake said.

'You can call me a lot of things, but you can't ever call me chicken,' Danny laughed.

'Unless of course you really need the eggs,' Sean quipped.

Danny groaned. 'What time are we rehearsing?'

'In ten minutes,' Snake replied. 'The rest of the lads are in the first dressing-room just down the corridor to your right. The floor manager will come and get you when they want you.'

'Are you not coming inside?' Danny asked.

'No.' Snake shook his head. 'I'm keeping an eye out for our "Snaps". I thought it would be a good idea to have our photographer, just in case the papers don't show up.'

'See you later,' Danny said, and he and Sean walked through the double doors leading to the studio. They turned right and found a dressing-room with a card on the door saying 'Poison Pig'.

Danny pushed open the door. Inside, Frankie, Richie, Frankie's girlfriend Carol, and Jeannie were sitting on the bench-style casual seating. Danny was surprised to see Jeannie, but his eyes mirrored Jeannie's joy at seeing him.

'Hello, Danny,' Jeannie said shyly. 'I hope you don't mind me coming along. I was going to ring.'

'It's fine,' Danny said, trying to hide the pleasure in his voice. 'So how are the crazy gang?'

'Crazy as ever,' Frankie laughed.

'How about you, Richie?'

Richie looked evenly at Danny, trying to gauge the extent of his reaction to Jeannie. In the two weeks that had passed since the fight, Richie knew Jeannie hadn't seen Danny at all.

'We'd better get changed,' Sean said, breaking the awkward silence. 'Snake said we're rehearsing in ten minutes.'

'We'll go to the canteen and get a cup of coffee,' Jeannie said, trying not to look at Danny as she headed for the door.

As the girls left the room, Danny and Sean unzipped their plastic suit-carrier bags. Danny quickly pulled off his jacket and shirt and took out a folded T-shirt from the zipped pocket of the bag. He opened it out and held it up for the rest of them to see. 'HUNGER MAKES ME FUCKING HORNY' was printed on the T-shirt in bold letters.

'Well, they won't miss that,' Frankie laughed.

Danny pulled the T-shirt on and looked at it in the mirror. He giggled at his reflection. Footsteps sounded outside the door and the handle moved as someone began to push the door open. Danny dived at the door and held it shut, pointing frantically at his jacket.

'Poison Pig? This is the floor manager,' a voice called.

'One second,' Danny said pulling on his jacket. He held the door with his foot pressed against it. When he had the T-shirt hidden, he pulled the door open.

'Sorry,' Danny said, 'I had no drawers on and we thought it was the girls coming back.'

'You should be so lucky,' the floor manager laughed. 'Anyway, five minutes, lads, fully dressed. I'll be back for you.'

When the door closed behind the floor manager, Danny let out a low whistle. 'That was fucking close.'

Danny quickly stripped off his casual jacket and put on the black kimono-style jacket he was wearing for the show. He closed the front over with the Velcro adhesive strip and beamed with satisfaction as he practised ripping it open, revealing the T-shirt underneath.

'It'll be bleedin' great,' Sean laughed. Danny and Sean quickly pulled on the rest of their gear. The floor manager was back almost immediately to lead them into Studio One. They tried to appear cool as they followed the floor manager around the heavy drapes at the bottom of the studio.

'This is your first time here, Richie, isn't it?' Danny was trying to establish rapport.

'Yeah,' Richie grunted.

'What d'you think?'

'It's smaller than I expected,' Richie said.

'So's your dick,' Sean laughed.

The floor manager put the band into position and called for quiet on the floor. He counted down from ten seconds and pointed at Danny to start.

At the back of the studio, Snake stood silently watching. All eyes were on the band. The studio had come to a stop, except for the four musicians and the three cameras. On the overhead monitors, Danny leered menacingly one moment and grinned boyishly the next, a quicksilver chameleon, taunting and teasing the cameras. When the band finished, the studio broke into applause. The stage hands, designers, sound technicians and the few stragglers who were involved with other guests on the show clapped Danny's masterful performance.

'That's not usual, lads,' the floor manager said. 'You couldn't get this crowd to clap for anything.'

After two more rehearsals, Danny and the band were relaxed and confident. 'OK, lads, thanks,' the floor manager said. 'We're happy with that. The director says he's very impressed with the performance, Danny, so see you back for the show. You're at the end of Part Two, just before the commercial break.'

Snake was waiting at the back of the studio for Danny and the boys to reach him.

'Brilliant!' Snake smiled. 'Absolutely brilliant! It's going to be magic. Pity we have to pull the stunt. It's nearly good enough without any gimmick.'

Despite the satisfaction of knowing they had done a good rehearsal, Richie's insides had turned to jelly. He could still feel the look that had passed between Jeannie and Danny. The little bit of magic he had been enjoying had vanished in that instant, the fresh pain blotting out all the memories of the good times.

'I'm going for a walk,' Richie said abruptly as he rose from his seat in the dressing-room and made a quick exit.

'Don't worry about him,' Sean said. 'I'll go after him.'

Frankie looked at Danny. 'Fancy a drink?'

'Not really,' Danny answered. 'I'm nice and tight and a drink might take the edge off it.'

'Yeah. Well me and Carol are going to pop down for one. Are you coming, Jeannie?'

'I'll buy you a cup of coffee,' Danny said gently.

'OK,' Jeannie said. 'Thanks, Frankie, but I'll stay with Danny.'

When Frankie had left, Danny looked at Jeannie.

'Well, we're alone at last. Except for our reflections in the mirror.'

Jeannie didn't answer. She just smiled back at Danny.

'I was a pig, and I'm sorry,' Danny said.

'It's all right,' Jeannie said. 'I know you were upset by the beating and everything.'

'No excuse,' Danny said. 'It was very uncool of me. Jealousy is a funny thing and it's certainly not improved by drink. Anyway, I felt badly enough about it that I haven't contacted you since. To be honest I didn't think you'd want to see me.'

'I was hurt more than angry,' Jeannie said. 'If you'd only known how much I had wanted to see you that Sunday, you'd never have said all those awful things to me.'

'Don't remind me!' Danny grinned ruefully. 'And you know what I did after I left you? I went and had more drink. And then more drink. I woke up the next morning in Snake's house, wondering how the hell I'd got there.'

Jeannie was laughing. Danny reached out his hand and

Jeannie raised hers to meet it.

'Friends?'

'Friends,' Jeannie replied.

'C'mon and I'll buy you that cup of coffee I promised you.'

Still holding Jeannie's hand, he pulled her to her feet. They stood very close together and then Danny tenderly leaned over and brushed his lips against Jeannie's forehead. Jeannie turned her face up to Danny and pushed her body against him. He felt himself go hard instantly.

'Let's get out of here,' Danny said. 'I have a dose of the old one-touch hard-on and I don't think this is the perfect place.'

Twenty-two

Sean and Richie sat on the perimeter wall of the television complex.

'Richie,' Sean said, 'I know it's none of my business, but are you in love with Jeannie?'

'You're right, it is none of your business.'

'Don't be such a pain in the hole, Richie. I'm only trying to be a friend.'

'So what if I am?' Richie said. 'She's in love with that stupid fucker. He has a beautiful wife at home that he obviously doesn't take care of, because she's out fooling around with Snake. Isn't one woman enough for somebody?'

Sean stared at the ground. He knew there was nothing he could say that would comfort Richie.

'Listen, Sean, I don't want to talk about it anymore. D'you mind if I'm on my own for a while?'

'Sure thing,' Sean answered, letting his legs slide to the ground. 'I'll see you back inside.'

Richie dug his hands deeper into the pockets of his jacket.

It was a cold night, but he felt numb rather than cold. A thick black cloud was settling in behind his eyes. He felt the dizzy sensation of panic.

'Breathe, Richie, breathe,' he told himself.

*   *   *

Danny sat with his back to the mirror, perched on the ledge of the counter top in the dressing-room. He swung his legs nervously backwards and forwards. He looked at the others. Richie was picking at his nails, moody and silent. Frankie was playing his guitar, his ear bent down to the unamplified strings. Sean was tapping out rhythms with his sticks on the metal leg of the bench seat.

A shuffle of feet sounded and the door burst open. The floor manager stepped into the room. 'OK, lads, we're on a commercial break, so we'll bring you into the studio now.'

The band followed him, treading carefully to avoid tripping over cables. The floor manager led them past the opening at the end of the black drapes and right around behind the audience until they came through another gap at the far end of the audience seating.

'You can hold on here,' the floor manager said. 'I'll get you a couple of minutes before the song.'

The members of the audience nearest to them looked at the band curiously. The black hair and the strange clothes made them look like futuristic undertakers.

The floor manager gave the signal for applause and the show recommenced with the host, Gay Byrne, welcoming a doctor who had written a book about cancer. It was a lively interview, with lots of audience participation.

Danny sensed the interview was coming to a close and seconds later the floor manager called them out and stood them on marked spots behind the mikes. Danny stood and looked at the audience, which had shifted its gaze from the interview to the band.

'All right, time for more music,' Gay Byrne, said. 'There's a band that has been causing ructions around town, with rude songs, but they are on their best behaviour tonight. Will you welcome four boys from Dublin who call themselves Poison Pig.'

The audience applauded and the sound of the opening bars of 'Designer Aid' came crashing through the speakers. The lights went down and the song began.

Danny felt the tightness in his throat and he could hear the hint of nervousness in his voice. 'Relax. Dance. Relax,' he told himself. He felt his juices flowing as he spun and whirled.

The other voices came thundering in on the chorus. 'Designer Aid, Designer Aid'.

Now Danny felt the power. He knew it was going well. He did a full spin, slowly enough to see Richie, Sean and Frankie all working hard throwing their own shapes. Danny grinned his evil grin, knowing he was in close-up. He stabbed his forefinger into the lens.

> *Goose the goose and stuff his craw*
> *We need lots more caviar to send to Africa ...*

The song soared into the key change for the last two choruses. Danny clenched his fist as the first chorus ended. The words of the final chorus tumbled out. He checked quickly to see that the camera was zooming back and then he stretched out his arms, quickly pulling them back in again, then ripping open his jacket to reveal the offensive T-shirt.

In the control-room the studio director reacted instantly, but it took several seconds before the cameraman obeyed the instruction to dip the camera lens to the floor.

The floor manager made to move towards the band and

then stopped as more instructions were relayed through his headphones. He turned to the host.

'We're in a commercial break,' he shouted. He turned back to the band. 'You guys, let's go.' Danny led the way, followed by Frankie, Richie and Sean. The audience began to boo as they passed.

'Dirtbirds!'

'Obscene!'

Danny and the band ran from the studio.

'That was a stupid thing to do,' the floor manager said to Danny.

'That's showbiz,' Danny said cheekily.

'Well, I don't think you'll be seeing much more showbiz here, mate.'

Inside the dressing-room, Snake was waiting behind the door. He scrunched up his face in glee and clenched his fists, smiling silently, letting them know the stunt had worked.

'It's OK, he's gone,' Danny said. 'Tell us, tell us?'

'It was fucking brilliant,' Snake said. 'The camera went all over the shop and then the screen went to black and it was like that for about five seconds until a commercial came on.'

'And what was the performance like?'

'Absolutely brilliant, all of you. It was fantastic. The whole country will be talking about it.'

'Did you hear the audience?' Sean said. 'My Jaysus, they weren't half aggro.'

'What was the reaction in the hospitality room?' Danny asked Jeannie.

'Well, they were all shocked, if that's what you want to hear. They were saying it's a disgrace.'

'Well, we're not going to win any popularity contests,' Sean laughed.

There were twelve people in the hospitality room when Danny led the band in. Three of them were staff and one more was pouring drinks. The rest were friends of the other guests on the show. As the band came through the door, there was silence and an awkward averting of eyes. Danny led the band up to the drinks counter.

'How 'ya doing?' Danny smiled. 'Can I have a vodka please?'

The hostess looked back at him, not knowing whether to smile or act cold.

'I only have white lemonade or tonic.'

'Tonic is fine,' Danny said. 'A vodka and tonic.'

The band got their drinks. They stood in a small cluster towards the back of the room and watched while the rest of the show continued. No one came near them.

When the closing credit of the show came up on the screen, Sean whispered: 'Now the crack starts.'

Three minutes later people began to trickle through the door. Some of them bridled at the sight of the band, and even though the room filled up quickly, the band stood isolated in an oasis of space, ostracised by guests and crew.

A security man appeared and approached them. 'Lads, I think it would be better if you all got out of here.'

Danny looked at Snake. A nod from Snake told Danny to follow. As they walked towards the door, the crowd melted to either side, except for one man, who barred the way. He lunged at Danny and grabbed him by the lapels.

Danny was completely taken aback by the sudden attack. In a split-second situation like this he had to make an instant decision whether he would bring his knee up into the man's balls or else head-butt him. He hesitated, a little unsure how to react.

'You're a cheeky, no-good pup,' the man roared, pushing Danny backwards.

Danny bumped into two men and a woman. The bigger of the two men saw his drink fly out of his glass. His face screwed up with rage. 'You punk bastard.'

He punched Danny hard in the mouth. Danny reeled back, clutching his mouth. Sean jumped in immediately and took a swing at the big man, but the security man grabbed his arm just as the blow was about to land.

Danny tasted the blood trickling inside his mouth. He could hear the flashbulbs popping and he felt dizzy and nauseous.

'Let's go. Let's go,' Snake said, grabbing Danny by the arm and hustling him out the door and along the corridor to the dressing-room. The others followed quickly after.

'How bad is it?' Snake asked.

'No teeth gone,' Danny said thickly, 'but it's fucking sore.'

Jeannie came rushing through the door.

'Are you all right, Danny?' she asked anxiously.

'One more time,' Danny grimaced.

'Let's get the fuck out of here as quick as we can,' Snake said. 'Leave your gear on. Just grab your stuff and I'll see you in the club. We have a table booked.'

The band gathered up the gear as quickly as possible and exited hurriedly through the swing doors. Four photographers were waiting. The flashbulbs started popping again and Danny pulled his bag up over his face.

'Show us the blood,' one photographer called.

'Bastards!' Danny swore, revealing his face with its bloodied and puffed lips. 'Sorry I'm not more badly hurt,' he hurled at them caustically.

'Danny!'

He turned to see Jeannie looking at him.

'Can I come with you?' she pleaded.

Danny flashed a look at Richie.

'Sure thing,' he said. 'Sure thing.'

Twenty-three

Danny woke without opening his eyes. In the brief instant between sleep and consciousness, his brain measured the potential severity of the coming hang-over and sent the message winging its way to every extremity of his body. His lips felt as if they were glued together and when he tried to lick them, tingles of pain caused him to blink fully awake.

The ceiling was unfamiliar, much higher than the ceiling of his own bedroom. Danny's brain raced. Where am I? How did I get here? What time is it?

He sat up very abruptly, unprepared for the thump of pain that came from behind his eyes. 'Sweet Jesus,' he shouted aloud, as the sudden stabbing assault seemed to spread into every corner of his head.

He felt a body stir beside him. He turned to see Jeannie's big eyes looking up concernedly at him.

'What's the matter?' she asked gently.

'If you're here, does that mean I'm still alive?' Danny asked thickly.

'Ooh!' Jeannie exclaimed 'Your lips look so sore!' She reached up a finger and touched Danny's bottom lip. Danny recoiled at the pain, hitting the back of his head against the headboard behind him.

'Aw, for fuck's sake,' Danny moaned. 'I'm getting bored with pain.'

Danny turned to Jeannie and slid back down under the bedclothes, gingerly easing himself onto the flat of his back.

Jeannie smiled at him.

'No jeering the afflicted,' Danny said. 'What time is it? How did I get here? And who are you?'

Jeannie laughed at Danny's last question, and slid her arm across his stomach.

113

'You drove, very crookedly. I don't know what time it is. And I'm Jeannie Callanan, the groupie.'

Danny looked askance at her as she spoke, but he could see by the smile on her face that she was making fun at her own expense.

The room was dark, with a hint of daylight slicing its way through a crack in the curtains. Danny suddenly felt the cold hand of panic clutching at his stomach. If he had been asleep all night, what would he say when he got home?

The night before came flooding back to him. Sean and Jeannie had travelled with Danny to the nightclub, but the evening had been frustrating and disappointing. Anyone who had been out and about hadn't seen the 'Late Late Show', so Danny's thick lips and Snake's uncontrolled euphoria were of little interest to those to whom they related the story.

Sean had had the good sense to insist that Danny ring Mary to let her know what had happened.

'Hi. It's me.'

'Well?' Mary said.

'You tell me,' Danny said. 'I got another box in the mouth in the hospitality room in RTE. Y'know when your screen went to black at home? Well, the punters in the studio started booing us and we had to clear out quickly from the studio.'

'And what did Gay Byrne say?' Mary asked.

'He didn't say anything,' Danny answered. 'I don't think he knew what was going on at the time, but afterwards when he found out, I think he was not very pleased. We went to the hospitality room after the show and it was crazy. Nobody would come near us, and eventually we were asked to leave, and as we were going out this guy lunged at me and this other fucker gives me a dig in the mouth.'

'Are you hurt badly?' Mary asked.

'Burst lips,' Danny said. 'Sore as a bastard, but I'll live.'

'Where are you now?'

'I'm in the club.'

'Where else?' Mary said coldly.

'Look, I'm just having a few drinks to unwind and then I'll be home,' Danny said.

'There's a few more of us could do with unwinding,' Mary spat into the phone.

*　　*　　*

Danny looked back to Jeannie lying beside him. She looked so young and fragile, not a line in her face, just a hint of eye make-up and the faint pink glow of her lips standing out from the pale white skin.

'Did we make love last night?' Danny asked.

'Kind of,' Jeannie answered. 'You fell asleep half way through it.'

'Did I wear a rubber?'

'You did,' Jeannie laughed. 'I think you used up most of your energy trying to get it on. You went on and on about AIDS and how I must take care of myself and then you spent ten minutes like a contortionist trying to get it on and by the time you did, it was too late and you gave up.'

Danny smiled ruefully. 'Do I get a second chance?'

'I'll consider it.'

'Where's Richie?'

'He went off somewhere when we were in the club and we never saw him again for the rest of the night. He was very moody and quiet all night.'

'D'you think it was because we were together?'

'Could be.'

'Has he been coming on strong to you?'

'Well, he's very gentle and kind and he puts up with my moods. And he brought me to the pictures. And we went for a few walks.'

115

'Did you sleep with him?' Danny tried not to let a querulous tone creep into his question.

Jeannie looked at Danny, full face.

'You, Danny, are the only man I have ever made love to.'

'Want to do it again?'

'Promise you won't fall asleep half way through,' Jeannie laughed.

'No chance.'

Danny pressed his lips to Jeannie's, but the pain made him wince.

'This will be a one-sided kissing job. I'll let my fingers do the walking instead,' Danny said, gently sliding his forefinger across Jeannie's lips into her mouth.

She sucked slowly on his finger, the moistness of her tongue sending shivers down Danny's back. He felt himself go hard instantly. He took Jeannie's hand and gently slid it down across his stomach.

'Danny, I love you,' Jeannie whispered, as she buried her face in his shoulder.

Twenty-four

Richie was cold when he woke. He was sitting in an old armchair which had the stuffing bursting through in several places. His brain felt numb and he shivered as he scrunched up his shoulders in an attempt to ease the stiffness.

Slowly he looked around the room. It was dirty and untidy. He could make out the shape of the two bodies in a camp bed, which was set against the wall in one corner of the room. On the floor, his friend Charlie was lying on his back in a sleeping bag, his mouth open in sleep, the whiteness of his face stark under the jet-black spiky hair.

The smell of dirty socks was heavy in the air. Clothes lay strewn haphazardly around the room. Along one wall, black plastic bags leaned awkwardly, spilling further clothes onto the floor. A grimy cooker and a tiny formica worktop leading to a battered aluminium sink took up a whole corner of the room. The heavy green curtains on the window hung limp with age and dirt and the paper peeled from the wall. In the small fire grate, the ashes of rolled up newspapers were evidence of the pathetic fire they had burned to combat the damp and cold.

Richie knew he must get away before Charlie and the couple in the bed woke. The night before he had needed them to give him a fix, but right now he needed to get away from everyone, especially from this dank room, which reminded him so much of the pain of his junkie days.

Pulling his comb from his pocket, Richie tiptoed out of the room and down the stairs. Dorset Street was bustling with Saturday morning shoppers. He began walking towards the bus stop and as he passed the newsagent's he saw the front page of the morning paper. It carried a three-column photograph of Danny, his hand to his mouth, reeling from the punch he had received the night before. In the background Richie saw his own face staring out white and sullen.

'Fuck it!' Richie said. 'Who needs it?' He turned his back on the newspaper shop and walked to the bus stop.

While the bus crawled down O'Connell Street, Richie wished he had taken the time to smoke a joint before he had left Charlie's. He hated the dizziness that came with his panic. It seemed to start in his stomach and push up towards his head. He fought the urge to jump off the bus and run through the crowded streets.

By the time he had switched buses and reached his flat in Rathmines on the other side of the river, Richie was shaking inside. He felt as if he was walking on cotton wool. He put the key in the door and turned it silently, opening it slowly and deliberately. As he closed the door behind him, he suddenly heard a voice coming from Jeannie's bedroom.

'Oh Danny! Oh Jesus! Oh Danny, Danny! I'm coming, I'm coming.'

A cold explosion of pain ripped Richie's body apart. He began to shake. Tears rolled uncontrollably down his cheeks. He turned and ran from the hall, slamming the door behind him.

In the bedroom, Danny heard the door slam. Jeannie was totally lost in ecstasy, her face a mask of exquisite pleasure as her body shuddered beneath him. He felt her relax and watched as a contented smile spread itself across her face.

'Did you hear that?' Danny asked.

'Hear what?'

'The door banging. Are you sure Richie isn't here?'

'Well, he wasn't here up to the time we went to bed last night.'

'Richie!' Danny called out. 'Is that you?'

'It must be the flat next door,' Jeannie said.

'Yeah!' Danny said relaxing into her arms. 'Anyway, you enjoyed that.'

'This time I'm certain I came,' Jeannie laughed. 'Can we do it again?'

'Not right now,' Danny said. 'I'd better get my arse home. I'll have to call by Sean's and make sure he gives me an alibi.'

He swung his legs out of the bed and padded to the bathroom, taking off the condom as he walked.

'Will I see you later?' Jeannie called after him.

'I'll have to wait and see.'

The water began to cascade from the shower. 'If you want to scrub my back, though, now is your big chance,' Danny shouted.

'I'll be right there, Master.'

*   *   *

Snake O'Reilly blessed his instincts as he listened to the playback of messages on his answering machine. It was rare for Snake to go to his office on a Saturday morning, but a hunch had prodded him awake at eleven o'clock and he had showered and got himself together remarkably quickly.

'This is Donie Horan in Tralee,' the voice on the machine said. 'What's the story on Poison Pig for next Friday night? Ring me as soon as possible.'

Snake smiled. He had tried to sell the band to the promoter already, without much success. Now it was obvious that the television appearance the night before had triggered a response.

Snake looked at the pictures of Danny on the front pages of the daily papers. If he played his cards right now, he could eliminate months of negotiations with record companies. If he could get the excitement up to fever pitch, one of the companies would be tempted to do a deal quickly and Snake would be ready. The lawyer in London had already got his instructions on what sort of deal to look for and Snake knew the key to increasing the pressure would be exposure in the British papers.

A sound of footsteps outside the office door made Snake look up. It was Richie. Snake could see he was extremely agitated. His hands were shaking, his eyes were flashing wildly and his clothes were rumpled from having slept in them.

'Richie,' Snake said, trying to make his voice sound normal. 'What brings you in here on a Saturday morning? There's never anybody here normally.'

'I know,' Richie said in a small voice. 'It's just that I called around to your flat and you weren't there, so I just took a chance and came here.'

'So what's up?'

'Well ...' Richie paused and nervously ran his tongue around his lips. Snake noticed the track marks of the tears that had run down Richie's cheeks.

'Are you in some kind of trouble?' Snake asked gently.

'I need some money,' Richie blurted out. 'It's not for me. It's a family problem, but I need some money and I need it quickly and I thought you would be the best person.'

Snake was staring at Richie, trying to figure out whether Richie was stoned or just badly upset. He tried to look closely at Richie's eyeballs. The eyes were wild, but the eyeballs seemed flat and dead.

'How much do you need?' Snake asked.

'About a hundred quid,' Richie said. 'Even fifty.'

'What sort of a problem is it, Richie?'

'I'd rather not say, Snake. It's private.'

'I have seventy quid in cash,' Snake said, pulling the money from his wallet. 'You can have that and I can stop it out of your wages next week.'

'Yeah, yeah,' Richie said, grabbing at the money. 'Thanks, Snake. I have to go now.'

'Where will you be later?' Snake called after him.

'I dunno,' Richie replied. 'Around.'

'Can I give you a buzz at home later?'

'Yeah, OK,' Richie said, scuttling through the door. Snake picked up the phone and dialled Frankie. He drummed his fingers while he waited for someone to answer. After a long time, a sleepy voice answered the phone with a hoarse whisper.

'Hello.'

'Frankie?'

'Yeah?'

'It's Snake. Listen, I'm sorry to wake you up, but I just had Richie here borrowing money from me and he looks and talks like he's very fucked up. D'you know what's going on?'

'I just know that he left us and wandered off last night and I didn't see him after about one o'clock,' Frankie croaked.

'Could he be back on the smack? Has he been showing any signs?'

'Jaysus, Snake, I don't really know. I haven't been paying that much attention. I think he was a bit fucked up last night because Danny and Jeannie went off together, but I thought he was only sulking a bit.'

Without replacing the receiver, Snake terminated the call and immediately dialled Sean's number. This time he didn't have to wait long.

'Flanagan's Funeral Home. Send us your stiff.'

'Hello, Sean,' Snake said. 'You're in good form this morning.'

'I'm always in good form,' Sean laughed. 'The world's happiest drummer.'

'Is Superstud with you?' Snake asked.

'He's right beside me, polishing his dick,' Sean chortled. 'Hold on.'

Danny came to the phone.

'Danny, can you come into the office?' Snake asked.

'Now?'

'Yeah, now. There are a couple of newspapers looking for you, but I think I'll keep them away, except for the English Sunday papers. If we can get a good spread in the English ones, we'll have the fuckers hopping on planes first thing Monday morning.'

'All right,' Danny sighed resignedly. 'It's just that I haven't been home yet and Mary will be bad enough without any more bullshit.'

'I'll ring Mary for you and tell her that I kept you out late and that I need you now in the office.'

'OK,' Danny said. 'I'll see you in about half an hour.'

'By the way, Danny, where will I say you stayed last night?'
'I stayed here at Sean's,' Danny lied.
'Sure, sure,' Snake said. 'See ya.'

Twenty-five

A smirk crossed Snake's lips. If Danny ever found out about himself and Mary it would be all over for Poison Pig. Danny deserves it, thought Snake. Does he think I'm so thick that I wouldn't have worked out that he was screwing Jeannie? Danny doesn't like me. So what? He's the same as the rest of them. They all want the notoriety and the money and Danny Boy is no different. Ego and greed. I know how to manage ego and greed and all I want is three hit singles and a hit album and then Poison Pig can take a flying fuck at itself. Besides, Mary is a great ride.

He dialled Mary's number.

'Hello.'

Mary was surprised to hear his voice. 'What are you doing ringing me at this hour of the day?' she asked.

'I'm just ringing to tell you that Danny is on his way into the office.'

'And where did he stay last night?'

'I rang him at Sean's,' Snake said.

'That doesn't mean he slept there,' Mary said.

'So how are you today?' Snake said, trying to defuse the anger in Mary's voice.

'I'm all right,' Mary said crossly. 'But while you're on, I'm going to tell you, for the last time, if you think you can come around here, fuck me and run off in an hour every time, you can forget it.'

The icy tone caused Snake to bluster. 'But ... but I thought you enjoyed it,' he said.

'Yeah, sure I enjoyed it,' Mary said bitterly. 'But did you ever hear of talk? You just want to stick your prick in somewhere, anywhere and then it's bye-bye and thank you ma'am.'

'But Mary, we agreed that Danny might walk in and that it would be better for me to leave.'

'Danny might walk in!' Mary spat sarcastically. 'I see his favourite groupie is in all the photographs with him again this morning.'

Snake glanced at the photographs in the papers. Jeannie's small white face was clearly identifiable, walking slightly behind Danny. He decided not to say anything. Jeannie was Danny's problem not his.

'Look, Mary, I'll make it up to you,' Snake said. 'We'll go for a long leisurely meal. We'll drive down to Wicklow or somewhere, where nobody knows us.'

'Sure, sure, Snake,' Mary spat. 'You'll keep your word as a man!'

Snake decided the conversation would not get any easier. 'I'll buzz you,' he said, replacing the receiver.

*   *   *

Snake snapped himself back to attention. For the next twenty minutes he concentrated on lining up phone interviews with the Irish editions of the English Sunday papers. The logic he used was simple. If the story was used on Sunday in the Irish editions, it could spill over into the British tabloids the next morning.

He also rang promoters and booked gigs for the following weekends. Snake was amazed at how readily they agreed to the big money he asked for.

'I want a one-thousand-pound guarantee against sixty-forty on the door.'

'I'll give you the grand flat, no percentages.'

Snake was thrilled to get the thousand. He knew now that he must keep the hype going. The record of 'Designer Aid' was in the shops. He guessed that after the television show it would start to sell.

The sound of Danny and Sean bounding up the stairs brought Snake up out of his chair. He walked around to the front of the desk as they entered the office.

'Front page pin-up,' Snake grinned.

'If I keep getting hit at this rate, I'll wind up as a centre-fold in the *Medical Times*,' Danny said ruefully.

'Yeah,' Sean chuckled. 'We'll have to stage a big festival in Wembley called First Aid.'

'So what's the crack?' Danny asked.

'Well, three big promoters have been on and we already have next Friday in Tralee, Saturday in Mayo and Sunday in Carlow, all at big readies.'

'Be Jaysus now, that's not bad!' Danny laughed.

'And I've lined up for you to talk to the Sunday papers.'

'Very impressive,' Sean smiled. 'Is there any bad news?'

'A bit,' Snake laughed. 'I think Mary is going to kick the shit out of you, Danny. She spotted Jeannie in the photographs in the papers.'

Danny looked at Sean.

'I think you'd better come with me when I go home, Magoo.'

'Me bollocks,' Sean said. 'I'm too young to die.'

'There's more bad news,' Snake said, bringing laughter to a halt. 'Richie was here a while ago, borrowing money from me. He was very fucked up.'

'What do you mean fucked up?' Danny asked.

'Well, he was all nervous and twitching and his hands were shaking and he looked like he had been crying.'

'What did he want money for?'

'He wouldn't tell me. He just said it was a family problem.'

'What do you think, Sean?' Danny said, his eyes betraying serious concern.

'I think it could be trouble, boys,' Sean said. 'I knew he was in weird form last night and he disappeared very quickly.'

'Did he go home?'

'Not as far as I know,' Danny answered, trying not to show annoyance at the way Snake had aimed the question at him, as if to suggest he was to blame.

There was a moment of tension, and then Sean broke the silence.

'It doesn't matter where he spent the night. The question is, what will happen if he goes back on the smack? God only knows where he's gone.'

'There's nothing we can do except wait until he shows up somewhere and hope we can talk him down,' Danny said. He turned and looked at Snake. 'What about the Baggot Inn this Thursday?'

'Snake O'Reilly says that this week's gig at the Baggot Inn will have at least half a dozen record companies from England,' Snake announced. 'I reckon we can hustle someone into signing a deal pretty quickly while the buzz is hot. But we have to keep the pressure up on the hype, so get on the phone there, Danny, and give these fuckers something to write about.'

Twenty-six

It was almost four-thirty when Danny swung the battered Citroen away from the kerb outside Snake's office. Danny's face was a mask of concentration until he was in the middle of the traffic. Then he turned to Sean. 'Have we any turf for a short patrol?' he asked.

Sean dipped into his shirt pocket and pulled out a small, tightly rolled piece of silver paper and unravelled it to reveal a small piece of hash.

'This won't exactly get us completely ripped,' Sean said, 'but it might give you the courage to face Mary, and it might give me some reason to explain to myself the stupidity of me going with you.'

'Shut up and fill the pipe,' Danny said. 'I'll do the same for you some day, when you're going home to a big, roarin' wife.'

Danny pulled the car in to the footpath outside his house. The two men climbed out and Sean followed Danny through the front door.

Mary was in the kitchen, sitting at the table. Danny could see from the way she was smoking her cigarette that she was agitated. He steeled himself for the abuse.

'Well, if it isn't the rock star! Are you just coming home to change your clothes or are you expecting to be fed as well?'

Danny heard Sean mutter an oath. He glared witheringly at Mary.

'This is my friend, Sean Devlin, who is *not* married to you.'

'He might as well be married to you,' Mary countered. 'He sees more of you than I do.'

'Very amusing,' Danny spat unsmilingly. 'Well, it just so happens that we had a major problem in the band.'

'What was that?' Mary sneered. 'Could nobody find the dope?'

Sean snorted, suppressing a laugh.

'If you must know,' Danny said, as if he were instructing an imbecile, 'Richie has gone missing, and there is every chance that he is back on the smack. We had to try and find him to straighten him out.'

'So you walked the streets all night searching for him?' Mary said sarcastically.

'Not all night,' Danny lied, 'but a fair part of it.'

'Did your little groupie friend help you look for him?'

'What are you talking about?'

'I'm talking about the little tart who keeps showing up beside you every time your picture appears on the front page of the paper.'

Danny threw a glance at Sean.

'I'm sorry you're in the middle of this, Sean,' Danny said. 'If you must know, Mary, she was with Richie and she just happened to be walking out behind me when they took the pictures. In fact, Richie and herself have been very close for the past few weeks and she is probably the reason why Richie is all fucked up in his head. Am I right, Sean?'

Sean took a deep breath and marvelled at the sheer brazenness of Danny's excuses. Now that he had been drawn into the argument, he had no course open to him except to endorse Danny's lies. 'It looks like it,' Sean muttered.

'And did she go on the search too?' Mary asked, arching her eyebrow.

'Of course she did,' Danny answered. 'She was more concerned than anyone else.'

'Well, I'm sure you were a great comfort to her,' Mary said acidly. Then she rose from the table. 'Can I have the car keys please?'

Danny handed them over.

'Where are you off to?'

'I think I'll go and search for Richie,' Mary said bitterly.

'Who knows, it might keep me out all night, and sure won't it give the kids a chance to get to know you.'

Mary walked quickly from the kitchen. Danny looked at Sean.

'Do you need a lift, Magoo? If you do, you'd better go now.'

'I will in me bollocks,' Sean whispered.

The door slammed and Mary was gone. Danny sank into a chair. Sean sat opposite him and shook his head as he saw a rueful smile spread across Danny's lips.

'Thanks be to Jaysus she's gone,' Danny said.

'I'll tell you something, you get the Nobel prize for lying,' Sean said. 'You were so convincing, I was starting to believe you.'

'It's the only way,' Danny said. 'I'll tell you something, though, it's tougher than doing a gig.'

Twenty-seven

The night passed slowly for Danny. He grew desperate for more dope. Once the kids were in bed, he searched every drawer and pocket hoping to find enough for a pipeful. He looked in every mug and bowl in the kitchen.

Suddenly his fingers closed around a small package of silver paper in a pewter mug on the dresser. Danny pulled it triumphantly from its hiding place. He looked at the long thin rolled-up shape, but didn't recognise it. He opened it up eagerly and was surprised to see that it contained not hash but a grey-white powder, finely chopped. Danny looked at the powder. He dipped the tip of his finger into it and licked it, pulling in his tongue at the sharpness of the taste, which he recognised as speed.

'Where the fuck did that come from?' he muttered, totally puzzled. He re-rolled the silver paper and, still staring at it quizzically, put it back into the mug. 'Pity I don't take speed,' he muttered.

Danny watched television fitfully, his mind wandering between the puzzle of the white powder and images of Jeannie. He pulled the phone to him to ring her number and then he remembered she had said she was meeting her friend to go to a movie. Instead he rang Sean.

'Dublin Centre for Wayward Girls,' came the cackle of Sean's voice.

'Could you please send me two wayward girls,' Danny laughed.

'Certainly, sir,' Sean replied. 'Any particular height or colour?'

'Black would be great,' Danny said, 'and if you don't have any black girls, a bit of black hash would do instead.'

'How's it going?' Sean asked.

'Edgy,' Danny replied. 'I'd sell me arse to a tinker for a bit of Bob Hope.'

'That's a heavy negative, good buddy,' Sean said.

'Fuck,' Danny sighed. 'What are you doin'?'

'I was just on my way out the door when you rang,' Sean answered. 'I'm going into Kehoe's for a drink and then I'll probably go to a club.'

'I wouldn't mind that myself,' Danny said longingly. 'Listen, keep your ears open and if there's any bit of Bob Hope stirring give us a ring and I'll organise some way to get it.'

'You got it, horse,' Sean said. 'Ten four, Big Ears.'

'And fuck you too, Noddy,' Danny said, putting down the phone.

Danny tried to read, but each time he got to the end of a page he realised he had absorbed nothing. He closed his eyes and thought of Jeannie and the night before. He slid his hand down inside the waist-band of his trousers and let it rest on his crotch. He felt himself get hard as the memory of the night before came back to him and, like a child clutching a worry blanket, he fell asleep holding onto himself.

*   *   *

The jangling of the phone brought Danny to his senses. He shook his head to clear it and a quick look at the clock on the mantelpiece told him it was just after midnight. Danny looked at the phone and decided it was either Mary ringing with more abuse or Sean to tell him he had found some dope.

He picked up the receiver.

'Hello.'

'Hello, Danny.'

Danny heard the tears in Jeannie's voice as she said his name.

'Jeannie. What's the matter? Where are you?'

'Oh Danny, it's Richie.'

'What about Richie?' Danny asked. 'What is it?'

'He's dead, Danny. Richie is dead.'

Danny took a sharp breath. 'What? Are you sure?' Maybe it was a coma.

'I'm certain, Danny, he's dead. His eyes look strange. He's definitely dead, Danny. Definitely.'

'All right, now calm down for a minute. Where are you?'

'I'm at the flat. Danny, can you please come over?'

'Yes. Yeah. But hold on for a minute. Where is Richie?'

'He's here in the flat. I went to the pictures after work and when I got home he was lying there with a needle in his arm.'

'Fuck, fuck, fuck,' Danny said away from the phone. 'Jeannie, handle it until I get there.'

'I can't go back inside, Danny. I just can't.'

'All right. Have you any money?'

'I have.'

'OK. Now here's what you do. Just close the door and get a taxi down to the club. Don't tell anybody what has happened, except Sean if you see him. Nobody else.'

Jeannie made no sound.

'Did you get that?' Danny said. 'Are you all right?'

'Yes, I'll be all right,' Jeannie whispered.

'OK. Do it now,' Danny said, 'and I'll see you in a few minutes.'

Danny replaced the received and stood up. He kicked the armchair. 'Sweet suffering Jesus!'

Twenty-eight

Danny had a cold feeling of guilt in the pit of his stomach but he galvanised himself into action. He rang Snake's number. There was no answer. Then he ran upstairs and looked in at the kids. They were sleeping soundly. Danny pulled on his jacket and took off down the street at a run. He had got as far as Francis Street before he managed to spot a taxi. He threw himself into the back seat and lay there panting as the taxi drove down Kevin Street and onto St Stephen's Green. He cursed himself for not leaving a note for Mary, in case she returned while he was out.

Jeannie's taxi pulled up directly behind Danny's. He was glad to see her before they went inside. She threw herself into his arms sobbing.

He tilted her face up to him. 'You'll have to be very together for a while, until we decide what to do. Do you think you'll be able to handle it?'

Jeannie looked at him with tearful eyes and nodded assent.

'OK,' Danny whispered. 'Let's go. Not a word to anyone.'

They walked to the door and Danny engaged in cheery banter with the doormen. Several people recognised him and stared at him curiously as he and Jeannie walked up the stairs. The club was crowded and Danny looked at Jeannie and made an instant decision.

'Stay put here,' he said, leaving Jeannie just outside the door. 'I'm going to see if I can find Snake or Sean.'

Danny fought his way through the crowd. It seemed like everybody he knew was there and they all wanted to talk about the 'Late Late Show'. Danny tried to peer over heads as he was stopped again and again. Snake was not at his usual table. He turned and fought his way towards the 'library'.

A great feeling of relief came over Danny as he suddenly saw Sean's smiling face through the crowd. He forced his way to Sean's side.

'Hey, my man,' Sean laughed. 'What's happening? Did we bust out of jail?'

Danny kicked Sean in the ankle and stared at him, trying to convey seriousness through his eyes. 'Have to see you outside. Trouble,' Danny hissed.

Sean started to open his mouth, but Danny stopped him with a hard stare.

Jeannie was still waiting outside. Sean looked at her tear-stained face and then looked quizzically at Danny.

'It's Richie,' Danny whispered. 'He's dead.'

'Sweet Jesus,' Sean breathed. 'When?'

'Jeannie found him at the flat about a half an hour ago with a needle in his arm.'

'Holy fuck,' Sean whistled. 'What are we going to do?'

'I was hoping I'd find Snake,' Danny said. 'You didn't spot him?'

'Not a sign,' Sean answered.

'That's fucking great,' Danny signed. 'Mary never came back, so I still have no car. We'll have to get a taxi to Leeson

Street and see if we can find Snake.'

'Well, let's go then,' Sean said.

The three of them went down the stairs, brushing past more well-wishers. They jumped into a taxi and sat silently in the back, afraid to talk in case the driver might hear what they were saying. Danny squeezed Jeannie's hand all the way, looking into her scared face every now and then, to reassure her.

The taxi pulled up on Leeson Street and Sean paid the fare as Danny and Jeannie crossed the road. They waited for Sean at the top of the steps and the three of them descended together to the basement club.

Danny called the manageress over.

'Is Snake here?'

'I ... I think he was here a while ago, but I'm nearly sure I saw him leaving,' she stuttered.

'Where was he when you saw him?' Danny asked.

'He was over there, but I'm nearly certain he's ... he's gone.'

'I'll have a look anyway,' Danny said, pushing his way through the throng at the bar. He stood on tip-toe, trying to see over the heads of the crowd. Then he crossed the dance floor and walked up the steps to the raised area at the back, where the tables nestled in several little alcoves. He came to the furthermost alcove and immediately recognised the back of Snake's head. Snake was pouring champagne, but from the way he was turned Danny could not see his companion.

'Snake!' Danny called.

Snake turned and, as he did so, he pulled his body around to reveal Mary, her glass outstretched for the drink. Snake's jaw dropped and Mary's smile hardened into a grim line across her mouth.

'You slithery little fuck,' Danny spat at Snake.

Snake started to rise. 'Wait, Danny, I can explain everything.'

Danny put his hand on Snake's shoulder and stopped him rising.

'You can explain nothing, you scumbag, and I'd like to beat the shit out of you right now ... but it'll have to wait, pal, 'cos we've got real trouble.'

'What do you mean?' The fear was bright in Snake's eyes.

'Richie's dead,' Danny hissed. 'A fucking overdose. Should be worth a few paragraphs in the paper, don't you think?'

Mary started to speak, but Danny stopped her with a wave of his hand.

'Don't say anything. Just get your arse home. I had to leave the kids on their own.'

Danny turned and crashed his way across the crowded dance floor, pushing people aside roughly.

'Did you find him?' Sean asked.

'Yeah, I sure did!' Danny growled. 'Pouring champagne for Mary.'

Sean hoped his eyes wouldn't betray what he already knew about Snake and Mary.

'*My* fucking Mary!'

Danny spotted Snake escorting Mary to the door. He intercepted them.

'Give me the car keys and get a cab,' he said roughly to Mary.

She gave him the keys without looking at him and as Snake led her to the door, Danny called after him. 'You get your arse back in here pronto.'

As they left, Mary raised her gaze and spotted Jeannie.

For an instant their eyes met and then Mary stepped quickly out through the open door.

Twenty-nine

When the ambulance had taken Richie away, Danny sat in the chair where his body had lain. In the stillness of the room he went over the events of the previous months. If he hadn't let Jeannie fall in love with him, would she have had a real relationship with Richie? Just how much had Richie been in love with Jeannie? Was the overdose a deliberate act to kill himself or just a cry for help?

Danny remembered all the things Jeannie had told him about Richie's attention to her, the trips to the movies, the visit to the zoo and he acknowledged to himself that he had noticed the hangdog look on Richie's face every time he and Jeannie had left his company.

What he would never know was that Richie had heard himself and Jeannie making love just hours before he took his fatal overdose.

Snake sat at the small formica table in the corner of the sitting-room, glowering across at Danny. In the hours that had passed since Danny had discovered Snake and Mary together in Suesey Street, the relationship between Danny and Snake had changed dramatically. Danny had become the master.

'If you as much as contact one newspaper, I will personally break your fucking neck.'

'Don't be so stupid,' Snake shot back angrily. 'Why should I want to contact the newspapers?'

'Because you're a greedy, no-conscience bastard with the feelings of a slug,' Danny snarled.

Jeannie broke the silence. 'Would anybody like another cup of tea?'

Sean, who had been dozing quietly at the other end of the couch, suddenly came awake. 'That's a great idea, Jeannie.'

'What about you, Snake?' Jeannie asked, glancing across at him.

'If you're making one I'll have a cup,' Snake said sullenly.

Danny looked at Sean. 'Have we any bit of dope at all, Sean?'

'I think I've got enough for one more joint and that's it.'

'I have a bit of hash,' Snake said.

Danny flashed him a bitter look. 'I don't want a fucking thing you have, Mister. Nothing.'

Snake finally snapped, pushing back the chair from the table. 'This is bullshit. I'm getting out of here. I'm not taking any more crap from you.'

He rose and stared levelly at Danny, before turning for the door. Danny was up from the couch like a panther, springing into the path between Snake and the door, his eyes blazing.

'You'll go nowhere, you prick, until I say so.'

Snake was alarmed at the ferocity of Danny's attack. He shrank back from Danny and went to sit back down again.

'Get out!' Danny shouted. 'Get the fuck out, you snivelling bastard! Get out before I fucking kill you!'

Snake scampered past him, clawing at the door handle to pull it open. Just as he got the door open Danny let go with a kick that landed square on the seat of Snake's tight pants.

'That's the best laxative Snake ever got in his life,' Sean laughed as Danny banged the door shut.

Danny let his shoulders drop. A smile creased his face. With Snake gone, the tension was dramatically reduced. He suddenly felt very tired and drained. Jeannie stepped towards him and put her arm out to touch the back of his neck with a soothing hand. He pulled away from her sharply.

'I was only trying to help,' she said quietly.

'I'm sorry,' Danny said. 'Just give me a few minutes, OK?' He turned to Sean. 'What about that joint, Magoo?'

'Coming right up,' Sean said, reaching into his pocket.

'And that nice cup of tea you promised us?' Danny said to Jeannie.

Danny slumped back into the couch, closing his eyes. What a mess! It was as if someone had pressed a button. He no longer wanted Jeannie. He didn't need her. He wasn't responding to the touch of her fingers. Whatever intimacy had been between them was gone. The thrill of her body had blinded him to the true nature of their relationship.

Danny marvelled at how quickly a life could be changed by one event. Richie's death had forced him to review the values that he lived by. His perspective on Poison Pig, on Snake, on Mary had gone through a total turnaround. He suddenly hated Poison Pig and everything it stood for. It was a cheap con job, and not alone was he part of it but he had let Sean become part of it as well. And now Richie was dead, and whether he liked it or not, Danny knew some of the blame must rest with him. But was blame too strong a word? He had asked Richie to let Jeannie share his flat but he hadn't asked him to fall in love with her. If Richie hadn't killed himself this time, would he have killed himself the next time something in his life didn't work out right? And Mary? What about Mary? Why Snake? What could she see in the crawling bastard?

Danny squeezed his eyes at the torment of imagining Mary making love to Snake. The pain made him clench his fists in anger.

'Jesus!' he shouted aloud.

'Holy shit!' Sean said. 'You nearly made me drop the stupid joint.'

'Sorry,' Danny said sheepishly, as Jeannie came running in alarm from the kitchen.

'It's OK,' Danny said. 'I'm just a bit fucked up by the whole business.'

'Relax, pal,' Sean said. 'Get that into you.' He passed him

137

a tightly rolled joint.

'Is there tobacco in it?'

'Afraid so, Danny. Only way to pad it out.'

'Aw, fuck it! Who cares about lung cancer?' Danny took the joint and stuck it in his mouth.

They sat in silence, passing the joint back and forth. Jeannie poured them tea. Danny and Sean were lost in their own thoughts, but Jeannie kept glancing at Danny as though she sensed that whatever had been between them had disappeared.

Eventually, Danny asked, 'Are you going to stay here tonight, Jeannie?'

'Tonight?' Sean laughed. 'This morning would be more like it. It's bright daylight outside.'

Jeannie looked at Danny. 'I don't think I could stay here on my own,' she said.

Danny knew that Jeannie wanted him to stay. And he knew that if he stayed, she would want him to sleep with her.

'Sean,' Danny turned to his friend. 'Could Jeannie stay in your place for today?'

'No problem,' Sean said.

Jeannie tried to hide her disappointment. She wanted Danny to hold her and reassure her, to assuage her guilt that she had contributed to Richie's death. But there was a sudden coldness between herself and Danny which she couldn't comprehend.

'Are you going home?' Sean asked Danny.

'Yeah,' Danny sighed. 'Might as well face it now.'

'I think you'd be better coming to my place for a while,' Sean said concernedly.

'Fuck it, no,' Danny said. 'It's my problem and it's about time I started dealing with things. All this other nonsense is just bullshit.'

A tear trickled down Jeannie's cheek as she watched

Danny rise from the couch. This was a Danny she didn't know. This was a stranger with pain in his eyes.

'Let's go,' Danny said, walking to the door.

As Jeannie and Sean went past him, Danny took a last look back at the chair where Richie had died. 'So much for rock 'n' roll,' he said.

Thirty

Danny sped through the deserted streets of the Coombe, and within minutes he was pulling up outside his house.

A young man appeared from behind his car, a pen and pad in his hand.

'Excuse me, Danny,' the man said. 'My name is Colm Boyle and I'm a reporter with ... '

'Fucking ambulance chasers! Can you not just back off?'

The reporter was surprised by the attack.

'I'm sorry about Richie, Danny,' he said. 'I really am. I'm a fan of the band and ... well, I'm just doing my job.'

Danny looked at him. He looked about his own age. He suddenly felt remorse for his anger. 'I'm sorry,' he said.

The reporter regained his composure.

'What's your reaction to Richie's death?' he asked.

'Waste,' Danny said. 'Terrible waste. Richie was a really nice young guy and a very talented musician with a great future ahead of him.'

'Did you know he was on heavy drugs?' the reporter asked.

'None of us knew,' Danny answered. 'We all knew he had a problem in the past, but he had been clean for a long time and it came as a great shock to us all.'

'Who found the body?'

'The girl who shared the flat with him.'

'Was he involved with this girl?' the reporter asked.

'No!' Danny snapped. 'They were just sharing the flat.'

'Do you think Richie's death had anything to do with the television show on Friday night?'

'Nothing whatsoever,' Danny said. 'The "Late Late Show" was a gig and Richie was part of the band.'

'Does anybody know where he spent his last hours?'

'None of us are sure,' Danny answered. 'He was with us after the show but none of us saw him yesterday.'

'What will happen to Poison Pig now?'

'That's something I haven't thought about,' Danny lied. 'I don't think any of us will think about it until after Richie's funeral.'

The reporter flipped his notebook closed. He was getting minimal co-operation from Danny.

'Thanks, Danny,' he said. 'I'm sorry for bothering you and I really appreciate it.'

'Sure, sure,' Danny said, putting his key in the door.

* * *

Danny let himself into the house. He could hear voices in the kitchen. He cursed. He wanted to be alone with Mary.

He heard Frankie call out. 'Is that you, Danny?'

'Yeah,' Danny answered, walking into the kitchen.

Frankie and his girlfriend, Carol, were sitting at the kitchen table. Mary was standing by the cooker, a teapot in her hand.

'How'ye,' Danny said, his voice sounding tired and grim.

'Would you like a cup of tea?' Mary asked.

Danny let his eyes meet Mary's. There was no animosity in them. She looked at him with the old softness, and he sensed that, like himself, Mary had been snapped back to reality by the tragedy of Richie's death.

'I'd love one,' Danny said, making sure there was no edge

to his voice.

'What a fuck up,' Frankie said, as Danny sat opposite him.

'You said it,' Danny agreed.

'I knew he was acting weird on Friday night,' Frankie said. 'He hardly spoke the whole time we were in the television station and he was as bad when we got to the club. And then he just disappeared.'

'Did you know he was back on the gear?' Danny asked.

'No,' Frankie said, shaking his head. 'I really thought he'd stayed clean. I thought he was just going through one of his wobbly periods, but I thought he'd pull out of it as usual.'

'Well he didn't, poor fucker,' Danny said. 'How did you find out? We couldn't find you last night.'

'Snake left a message this morning. He banged on my door and stuck a note under it,' Frankie said.

'And he didn't talk to you at all?' Danny said, arching his eyebrow.

'Does Richie's old man know?' Frankie asked.

'Yeah,' Danny told him. 'He came over last night.'

'Did he see the body?'

'Yeah.'

'And what did he say?' Frankie asked.

'Not a lot,' Danny replied. 'He's a cold bloody bollocks.'

'So what happens now?' Frankie asked.

'Well, there'll be a post mortem, I'd say today or tomorrow, and the body will probably go to the church tomorrow.'

'Jesus, it's going to be rough on his brother and sisters, especially following so quickly after his Ma,' Frankie said.

'Sure is,' Danny agreed, realising that he hadn't spared a thought for the other members of Richie's family.

They sat in silence for a while and then Danny said, 'Listen, Frankie, can I catch up with you later? I'm absolutely wrecked and I need to get some kip.'

'Sure thing,' Frankie said. 'Where will I see you?'

'What about the Foggy Dew at about eight o'clock? And try not to talk to too many people about it. I've just had a reporter jumping at me outside the door before I came in.'

'Outside here?'

'Don't worry, he's gone now.'

'See you later.'

Mary came back in, having seen Frankie to the door. She looked at Danny and sat opposite him. They gazed at each other for a few intense seconds and then in one movement they each stretched out a hand to touch across the table.

'How did we get into such a mess?' Danny said softly.

'I don't know,' Mary said.

'It's so stupid,' Danny said. 'We have one each other, we have wonderful kids, we have a house, we have our health.'

Mary looked at Danny, tears springing to her eyes. She squeezed his hand.

'Why?' Danny asked.

'I don't know,' Mary answered. 'You didn't seem to care. You were never here and you never told me what was going on.'

'But you knew what was going on,' Danny said.

'No, I didn't,' Mary said. 'If it wasn't for him I wouldn't have known anything about what was happening to the band.'

'And was he coming here when we were out playing and recording or whatever we were doing?' Danny asked.

'Sometimes,' Mary nodded.

The piece of silver paper he had found in the mug on the dresser suddenly clicked in Danny's mind.

'Was he giving you speed and coke, while he was coming here?'

Mary nodded again.

'The slimy bastard. If he ever lays another finger on you ...'

'He won't,' Mary whispered.

They sat silently, each staring at the table surface, Danny scratching at imaginary flecks of dirt, Mary glancing up at him every few minutes. Finally she spoke.

'What about you and that girl?'

Danny didn't look up as he answered. 'Ego. Just another stupid man satisfying his stupid ego. No more, no less.'

'Do you love her?' Mary asked.

This time Danny raised his eyes to look at Mary.

'No. I thought I did, but I swear to you, I don't.'

They squeezed each other's hands and exchanged rueful smiles across the table.

'Can we start again?' Danny asked.

Mary nodded.

'I love you,' Danny said.

'And I love you too,' Mary smiled.

Thirty-one

Monday morning's papers had Richie's death on page one. The English tabloids had also picked up the story 'REBEL ROCKER'S DRUG OVERDOSE'.

'Some rebel,' Snake snorted to himself, as he put the paper down on his desk. He was extremely agitated. The last two days had been a roller-coaster. The high of the television had not had time to percolate through his body before Danny had caught him with Mary. And then, Richie had died.

The most extraordinary aspect of Richie's death was the amount of interest it had sparked in the record companies in London. All morning Snake had fielded phone calls from London – and two calls from New York.

'Is this Snake O'Reilly?' a voice had twanged.

'Yes'

'Hi, this is Tony Cannelli from Azcade Records in New York. We hear you got a hot band there in Poison Pig.'

'Who told you about the band?' Snake asked.

'Snake,' the voice said, 'when you're hot, you're hot. Who doesn't know about it?'

Snake shook his head in bewilderment. 'So what can I do for you?'

'Tell me about the band?'

'Well, would it not be better if I sent some tapes and photographs so that you could ... '

Snake didn't get a chance to finish.

'When will the band be playing next?' Cannelli asked.

Snake's brain was racing. He didn't know if the band would ever play again.

'Why do you want to know?'

'We'd like to get some of our people over to have a look at you,' the voice said.

Should he take a chance? Would he be able to talk Danny into playing? Would he be able to pull it off this week? Snake got excited at the thought.

'We'll be playing a benefit memorial gig for our bass player who died over the weekend ... '

'Yeah, we're real sorry about that.' Cannelli's voice was sincere.

'So that will happen on Thursday in Dublin,' continued Snake, growing in confidence, 'but you'd better call to confirm tomorrow.'

'Sure thing,' Cannelli said. 'Ciao for now.'

Snake put the phone down and let his breath whistle through his lips. Death was obviously a hot commodity. If he could pull off the gig, it would be like the famous Rolling Stones concert in Hyde Park two days after the death of Brian Jones. This would be the rock 'n' roll story of the year, if the cards were played right.

He picked up the phone and dialled.

'Hi. I'm looking for Owney Grace,' Snake said.

'You're talking to him. Who wants him?' came the abrasive response.

'This is Snake O'Reilly, manager of Poison Pig.'

'Oh yeah,' the voice said. 'I knew Richie. I'm sorry about that, man.'

'Thanks, Owney,' Snake said. 'Look, we think ... that is, we'd like to be able to make our gig in the Baggot Inn this Thursday a sort of memorial gig for Richie and I was wondering if you might be free to play? Have you something on at the moment?'

'Well, I've a couple of things – but, eh, yeah I'd like to do it. When could we rehearse?'

'I'm not a hundred per cent sure yet,' Snake said. 'I'll ring you later on this evening.'

'OK. That's cool.'

'Owney,' Snake slipped into his slithery mode, 'we also have several big gigs at the weekend and the bread would be really good.'

'If the bread is good, I'm your man,' came the reply.

'OK.' Snake said. 'Talk to you later.'

Snake put the phone down. He clenched his two fists and pounded the table. 'I've got to pull this off,' he whispered.

Snake called his secretary into the room. 'I want you to ring Danny Toner and tell him there is a band meeting today at four o'clock and that it's very important that he is here for it.'

'Is that it?' she said.

'Tell me when you get him and then I'll tell you what else to do.'

The secretary left the office and Snake looked at his diary. He had already confirmed the dates for the weekend and he knew from instinct that by the end of the day he would have enough dates to make Poison Pig a very worthwhile investment. All he had to do was hold them together.

The secretary stuck her head in. 'I got Danny Toner.'

'Himself?' Snake queried.

'Yes,' she replied.

'What did he say?' Snake asked.

'He said he wouldn't miss it for the world. Then he hung up.'

Snake rang Sean. With masterful slyness he began to exude his poisonous charm.

'The gig would be a gesture to Richie, Sean.'

This bastard is trying to manipulate me, Sean thought. He's hoping that I can bring Danny onside. Slimy shit.

'Yeah, I know, Snake, but I don't think Danny will do it.'

'Look, Sean, I know you all think I'm a bastard, but Richie deserves a bit of a tribute. You are the most sensitive member of the band. You understand. If anyone can talk Danny into it, you can.'

'I'll have a shot, but I wouldn't count on it, Snake.'

'I'll see you at the meeting, Sean. Four o'clock.'

Snake was pleased with the line he had taken with Sean. He dialled Frankie's number.

'Hello, Frankie. It's Snake.'

'Yeah, Snake.'

'Listen, Frankie, I'm sorry that I didn't see you since Richie died, but I suppose you heard about the other hassle as well?'

'You mean you and Mary?'

'Yeah,' Snake said. 'So I was lying low. Terrible shock about Richie wasn't it?'

'Desperate,' Frankie replied. 'Can't believe it. If only I'd known he was that fucked up.'

'If only we'd all known,' Snake said insincerely. 'Anyway, Frankie, there's a band meeting at four o'clock here in the office, you and me, Danny and Sean. We have a few things to sort out.'

146

'Yeah.'

'And listen, Frankie, one more thing. I was talking to Sean, and he agreed with me that it might be a good idea to try and do the Baggot on Thursday as a memorial gig for Richie. How would you feel about that?'

'Were you talking to Danny about it?'

'Not yet. He isn't home at the moment, but I talked to Sean. Maybe you should give Sean a ring and we can all bring it up with Danny?'

'I suppose so,' Frankie said hesitantly.

Everything was going too fast for Frankie. One day everything was brilliant, he was on television, he was playing with a hot band, he could hear himself on the radio. Now everything had turned to shit and the whole future of the band was in jeopardy. And it was all outside his control. All he wanted to do was play his guitar and not get involved in any hassle. What should he say to Snake? Should he ring Danny before he gave an answer? And wasn't it Danny who had helped create this mess anyway?

'Listen, Frankie, as the real rock 'n' roller of the band, you know it would be a cool gesture.'

'Yeah, I think you're right, Snake.'

Thirty-two

For the next few hours, Snake lived out his prediction, filling the diary with dates for the next six weeks. In between, the calls kept coming from newspapers, from record companies and from music publishers in London. Snake told them all about the gig the coming Thursday.

Snake looked at his watch. A quarter to four. He reached for his wallet and pulled out a small flat white package. He opened it carefully and poured a small mound onto the sleeve of the album which lay on his desk. He slipped out a credit card and chopped at the white powder and when he had the package refolded and tucked away again in the wallet, he pulled out a wad of money, selected a crisp twenty-pound note, rolled it tightly and poked one end into his right nostril and the other to the tip of the long thin line of coke.

Snake sat back, massaging his nostrils and running his fingers along the remains of the powder on the record sleeve. He rubbed his fingers along his upper gums. After a few minutes he felt the numbness on his gums and he felt the familiar odd feeling in his nose. Snake liked the bright clear buzz that the coke brought with it. He was going to need some help to deal with Danny.

Danny and Sean arrived together. They stayed in the outer office until everybody had coffee. Then Snake called his secretary.

'Angie, no calls, no callers. Take messages and get home numbers if necessary. And would you ask the boys to come in?'

The door opened. Sean stepped into the room, followed by Frankie and Danny. Behind his desk, Snake tensed himself, expecting Danny might spring to the attack.

Snake got up from behind the desk and came around to the front of it. Danny stood with his back to the door, looking balefully at Snake. Sean could feel the hostility crackling in the air. Snake pulled his gaze from Danny and looked at Sean and Frankie as he began to speak.

'I did something with Danny's wife, which I am not proud of. It wasn't something that a mate would do and I have no excuse other than that his wife is a beautiful woman. If I could turn back the clock I would, but I can't, so we have to go forward and try not to make the same mistakes again. All of us here have worked very well together for the past few months and it's stupid that I am the one who should fuck it up. You guys have the talent and without you there is no gig for me. I know that you think I am a sneaky bastard, but I've worked hard for all of you and with you, and I want to offer my humble apology to Danny in front of you two and I also want to say that I hope we can go on working together.'

Snake finished the speech he had been rehearsing for hours. He was proud of himself.

Nobody spoke for what seemed like an eternity. Sean looked to Danny for some reaction, but he was staring at the ground.

'How about it, Danny?' Snake said softly, stretching out his hand in Danny's direction.

Danny raised his eyes from the floor, letting them travel slowly up Snake's body. He looked at Snake, then at Sean and then at Frankie and with a slight step forward, he shook Snake's hand, firmly but briefly.

The atmosphere became more relaxed and everybody found a seat. Snake walked back behind his desk. He could feel the cool clear high of the coke and he was inwardly exulting at the success of the first stage of his mission.

'I suppose you all saw the papers?' Snake said.

All three nodded.

'Then I don't need to tell you that everybody knows who Poison Pig are now. I've even had calls from America today. I've had so many enquiries about the band today, you'd swear we were U2.'

'Maybe we should run down to the morgue and tell Richie the good news,' Danny spat.

'I'm sorry. I didn't mean to ignore Richie's death, I was just wondering about whether you'd seen the papers. That's all.'

'But it's true what I said, isn't it?' Danny continued.

Snake looked at him levelly. 'You are right to an extent, but don't forget we organised the stunt for the television show and pulled it off successfully. We'll never know just how far that would have taken us because it's all mixed up now.'

'So Richie's death is a kind of bonus,' Danny said.

'I didn't want Richie to die any more than you did,' Snake countered. 'I'd be much happier if Richie was alive. He was a good musician and a great performer and sadly for him, it was the only thing he was able to handle in his life. But I didn't kill Richie.'

'Nobody killed Richie,' Sean interjected.

'I didn't mean it like that,' Snake said. 'I apologise. I take it back. What I am trying to say is that there is nothing any of us could have done to save Richie. But he is dead, and we are still here, so if Richie's death can help us, then it's Richie's way of still being in the band.'

'Jesus, I'm going to puke,' Danny shouted.

'Danny,' Snake was leaning over the desk towards Danny, adrenalised beyond fear. 'We shook hands on something a few minutes ago, but you're still letting it get in the way of what we are talking about here, the future of Poison Pig.'

Danny looked back at Snake scornfully. 'So what is the great future of Poison Pig?'

'I'll tell you what it is,' Snake said. 'The future is four record companies from England and two from America ready to come to Dublin right now. The future is every newspaper in England wanting to do a story on the band and especially the next gig. The future is a live recording of our next gig, which we release as a tribute to Richie. We pay for it, therefore we own the master tapes. We sell it to the highest bidder or to the bidder who will do us the most good. As long as we own it, we call the shots. And we can do our own publishing deal and get money up front on both deals.'

'Jesus, but you're a cynical, conniving bastard,' Danny said.

'There we go again,' Snake bristled. 'This is rock 'n' roll,

Danny. This is the world we are choosing to make our living in. These are the rules of rock 'n' roll. So live by them. We've been working for months to get our gig going. I had to pull all kinds of strokes, with newspapers, photographers at hospitals, the guy in the hospitality room at RTE.'

'What guy?'

'The one who blocked your way. The guy who hit you was a real punter, which made it brilliant.'

Danny looked at Snake incredulously. 'Are you telling me, Snake, that you were responsible for the photographers showing up at the hospitals and ... '

Snake cut across him. 'What are you, Danny, some kind of innocent? Lots of bands have hassles, but you never hear about them because they don't know how to get the mileage. If all those guys hadn't thumped you, we'd have had to hire somebody to do it.'

'Boy, Snake, you are some operator! Here I am, a trained monkey and I never spotted it. I must be slipping.'

'You get nothing for nothing,' Snake said. 'I know better than anybody the value of good manipulation of the press.'

Danny went icy calm inside. He hoped his eyes wouldn't betray him as he mentally lashed himself. He couldn't believe that he hadn't spotted all of Snake's moves. Wasn't he the loud-mouth who had told everybody he was in complete control and well able for Snake? What must Sean think of him? And did Mary know about all the subterfuge without telling him? He kept his face a mask. He must listen carefully to what Snake had planned and then he would know what to do. Most of all he must let Snake continue to believe that he was in total control.

'OK,' Snake said. 'Here's what I think we should do. The interest in the band is so hot at this moment that I think we should do Thursday in the Baggot Inn as a memorial gig for Richie.' He turned to Danny. 'I spoke about this to Sean and

Frankie already, but we all agreed that you should have the final say on whether we should do it or not.'

Danny stared back at Snake and said nothing, his brain racing at a million miles an hour. He could see that Snake had already used his persuasive powers to swing Frankie and Sean to his way of thinking.

'It'll be like the Stones gig after Brian Jones died,' Snake spluttered. 'Can't you see it, how massive it will be?'

Danny looked back at Snake, fighting down his anger.

'Sounds great all right,' he lied. 'What do you guys think?' he asked, looking at Sean and Frankie.

'It'll be good,' Sean said, trying to read Danny's expression.

Danny looked back levelly at Sean, nodding to him a message to stick with him.

'Great rock 'n' roll,' Frankie said.

'So who do we get to replace Richie?' Danny asked.

'I was thinking about Owney Grace,' Snake answered. 'He looks good and he's a great bass player.'

'He's also a big-headed bollocks,' Sean interjected.

'Too true,' Danny agreed.

'Look, we need somebody who is good and who can learn the stuff fast,' Snake said. 'I'll have a word with him about staying cool.'

'Will you get in touch with him?' Danny asked Snake.

'Yeah, leave it to me,' Snake said. 'When will I tell him to be ready to rehearse?'

'Tell him tomorrow at ten o'clock,' Danny said. 'Is that cool for you guys?'

Sean and Frankie nodded their assent.

'And if he works out, should we go ahead and do the weekend dates?' Snake added cautiously.

'Why not?' Danny smiled.

'The bread is good,' Snake said.

'That's all that matters,' Danny said, hiding his sarcasm

behind a huge smile. 'Let's go, lads. I want to talk to you about something.'

Snake allowed himself a self-congratulatory smile as the three men left his office. He clicked the door shut. 'It's in the bag,' he whispered. 'It's in the bag.'

Thirty-three

Danny, Sean, Frankie and Richie's young brother, Colin, carried the coffin from the hospital morgue to the hearse. Snake stood sullenly to one side, knowing, without having to be told, that any attempt by him to assist would be met with hostility from Danny.

Richie's family stood in a pathetic cluster. His father's eyes had a forbidding stare, cold and hostile. Beside him, Richie's two sisters looked bewildered.

Danny watched from a distance. He could see that people were afraid to approach Richie's father. He walked to the family group purposefully.

'Is there anything I can do to help?' Danny asked.

'There's nothing any of you people can do now,' Richie's father replied, in a voice that was cold and reproving.

'We would like, if you'll agree, to play some music at Richie's funeral mass. It has become a sort of tradition here now to do that.'

'Why can't you leave him alone, now that he is dead?' Richie's father said. 'It was this wild rock music that killed him.'

Danny reacted angrily inside, but stopped himself in time from exploding. He spoke quietly. 'Whatever else killed Richie, it wasn't the music. The one place that Richie was completely happy and able for his life was on stage. I don't think you ever saw him play, so you probably don't know, but he was very talented and very popular. People loved Richie. He was quiet and shy, but I can tell you that he was liked for his gentleness and his sensitivity. The best way that we can show how much Richie's death has upset everybody is to let his friends play a bit of music.'

Richie's father's eyes betrayed no emotion. 'If you think that is what should be done, you do it, but leave me out of it. I didn't understand these things when my son was alive and I don't expect to understand now that he is dead.'

Danny wanted to shake the man. He wanted to point at the coffin and shout at him. *Look, that is Richie. Can't you even say his name? Richie! Can you not say that you loved him? That you're sorry that he is dead? Can you not cry, fuck you?*

Instead, Danny motioned to Sean and Frankie and the three of them climbed into Danny's car and followed the hearse as it began the journey to the church.

'Anybody fancy a toke?' Sean asked.

'I would murder a joint,' Danny said. 'Even better, I'd murder a pipe.'

Sean took the pipe from Danny and began to fill it with small pieces of hash.

'Where the fuck did you get that?' Danny asked.

'Never you mind,' Sean said jokingly. 'I knew we would need a lot between today and tomorrow so I grabbed it when it was going. You'll owe me thirty quid when I dole it out.'

They smoked the pipeful of hash in silence, as the small funeral cortège wound its way through the evening traffic.

'Jesus, Richie's Da is pathetic,' Danny said, breaking the silence.

'Unbelievable,' Sean agreed.

'Frankie, you knew Richie years ago, didn't you?'

'Yeah,' Frankie said.

'Was his Da always like that?'

'From what I can remember, he was. I know that Richie used to be scared of him because he was always getting on his case about not having a sensible job and a career.'

'What chance have those kids got?' Danny said. 'The poor little bastards have nobody to turn to for comfort. I very nearly blew my cool with him. I was just about to let fly, but I said, fuck it, it'll only upset the kids even more.'

'Did you ask him about playing in the church?' Sean asked.

'Yeah, he said it would be all right, but it had nothing to do with him. As far as he is concerned, rock 'n' roll killed Richie.'

'That's him all right,' Frankie said.

'So what'll we play?' Sean asked.

'Well, it can only be acoustic guitar and the organ. Frankie, you tell us what would be good on two guitars?'

'Yourself and myself?' Frankie asked.

'Yeah,' Danny said. 'Something that's suitable. What about "I Shall Be Released"? Richie was a great Dylan freak.'

'That's a great idea,' Sean said. 'D'you know it, Frankie?'

'Yeah, yeah,' Frankie said. 'We can have a blow on it later on, Danny, can't we?'

'I also think we should do "Crazy Dreams",' Danny said. 'I know it's not our thing, but Richie was always singing it to himself and I know he just worshipped Paul Brady when he was younger.'

'Will that be enough?' Sean asked.

'I think so,' Danny said. 'Especially if Richie's Da isn't too keen on the idea.'

Thirty-four

Jeannie stood in the middle of the huge crowd outside the church waiting for the funeral to arrive. She searched the faces for Danny, but she couldn't see him anywhere. She hadn't seen him since he had dropped her off at Sean's the morning after Richie's death. He had sent messages to her through Sean that he was caught up in arrangements for the band and for the funeral.

So much had happened that Danny didn't know about. Her parents had arrived at her flat, her father boiling with anger, fulminating about drugs and sex, while beside him her mother stood crying tears of relief to see that Jeannie looked all right.

'You pack your things and come with us right now,' her father said.

Jeannie stared at her father.

'I am eighteen years old and I will do what I like now,' she said evenly. 'Richie, who is dead now, was my friend and he died right here in this flat. He was just a nice guy, but you think he was some kind of freak.'

'He was a drug addict.'

'He was a victim,' Jeannie said quietly, 'and a lot of his problems were because he had a father who couldn't talk to him without shouting at him.'

She saw a flicker of hesitation in her father's eyes.

'I ran away because I couldn't take the shouting and the rows anymore. Don't you understand that? Don't you think that I miss you and Mam? But I couldn't stay there and put up with it anymore.'

Her mother stepped forward and wrapped her arms around Jeannie. Jeannie felt the tears spring from her eyes. Then her father's arms were around both of them and Jeannie could scarcely believe it when she saw tears coursing down his cheeks.

'Will you come home, love?' her mother asked.

'Not right now, Mam,' she answered tenderly. 'Let me go to the funeral first and then I'll see what I'm going to do.'

'But are you all right here in this flat on your own?'

'Yes, Mam,' she lied. 'I'm fine. This is the way I want it.'

Danny. If only Danny would come and stay and hold me tight and make me feel safe, she thought.

The hearse came into sight and behind it Jeannie saw Danny's battered car. She felt her stomach tighten. Would Mary be with him? Would he talk to her? She still felt a gnawing need to talk to Danny, to tell him again how much she loved him, in case he didn't understand. She wanted to feel the grip of his fingers, a solid union of the flesh that would say more than all the words she could think of.

She watched as Danny, Sean and Frankie took up their positions and carried the coffin inside the church where it would remain until the funeral in the morning. As he passed her, she caught Danny's eye. He looked at her and gave her a small nod, with just a hint of a smile and then he was swallowed up by the crowd following behind the coffin.

The prayers lasted for fifteen minutes. Jeannie remained in her pew as the crowd filed slowly from the church.

As the church emptied, Jeannie saw Danny, Sean and Frankie follow the priest in behind the altar. She sat in the quiet of the church as the last stragglers made their way to the door. When everyone had gone, Jeannie rose hesitantly and walked up the church to where Richie's coffin rested on a trolley in front of the altar. Jeannie genuflected and as she stood, she reached out a hand and touched the coffin.

Flipping open her bag, she pulled out a single red rose and placed it on top of Richie's coffin. Jeannie could not stem the flow of tears that coursed down her cheeks. She sobbed quietly, looking around to make sure no one was watching.

Minutes later, Danny, Sean and Frankie came walking around the altar and down the centre aisle. The three men spotted Jeannie simultaneously. Sean and Frankie walked on, but Danny stopped as he drew abreast of Jeannie.

'Hi,' Danny said softly.

'Hi,' Jeannie said, giving him an awkward smile.

'We were just going for a drink,' Danny said. 'Would you like to come?'

Jeannie nodded and followed him outside.

'Where do you want to go?' Danny asked Sean and Frankie.

'We could get a bus somewhere if you want to,' Sean said.

Danny flashed Sean a look, letting him know that the last thing he wanted was to be alone with Jeannie.

'Not at all,' he said. 'Will we go down to the Yacht, down there on the coast road?'

The chatter in the car was nervous. The tension between Danny and Jeannie was palpable. As they pulled up outside the pub, Danny turned to Sean and Frankie.

'You guys go ahead, I want to have a word with Jeannie. Order me a vodka and tonic and whatever Jeannie is having.'

'A glass of lager, please,' Jeannie said in a small voice.

Danny waited until Sean and Frankie had entered the pub before he spoke.

'So, how'ya doin'?' he asked.

'I'm all right,' Jeannie said, looking at him tearfully.

She suddenly let go and tears tumbled down her cheeks. She threw herself across into Danny's arms.

'Oh, Danny,' she sobbed. 'I've missed you. Will you come home with me tonight?'

'But you're staying with Myra, aren't you?'

'Yes, but she won't mind. I have my own bedroom.'

Danny stared coldly past Jeannie's head, which was nestling on his shoulder. His brain was icy clear. He tried to make his voice sound warm and caring.

'I can't, Jeannie. I have a lot of things to organise for the funeral tomorrow and then I have to go home.'

'My parents came up to Dublin.'

She watched Danny's eyes.

'It's OK, I didn't tell them anything about us. They want me to go home with them.'

'And what did you say?'

'I told them I had to get the funeral over with first before I knew what I was going to do.'

'And what are you going to do?'

Danny's question fell with a thud between them.

Jeannie raised her face and looked at Danny.

'Danny! Are we finished?'

Danny's stared straight ahead through the windscreen.

'Jeannie, I think you are a really bright and lovely girl. I am very fond of you and I really want to stay friends with you, but we can't be lovers anymore. I don't know how Richie's death affected you, but it made me think about all the things that are important to me and even though I loved every minute I was with you, I was only screwing up my own family. I have a responsibility to my children and I do love Mary.'

Jeannie pulled away from him.

'Even though she's been having an affair with Snake?'

'Jeannie, in case you didn't notice, I was having an affair as well.'

'But Mary doesn't love you. I'm the one who loves you.'

'Listen, Jeannie, I don't want to sound like some fucking priest or your father, but as you get a bit older you will find out that people can lose sight of what they have and it takes a shock like what happened with Richie to bring it all back into focus. I married Mary because I wanted to be with her and I think she married me for the same reason. Even though it is going to be shaky enough for a while, I think we can get our act back together. You have plenty of time to fall in love again. I'm just sorry that I have fucked up your brain a bit. It was pretty selfish of me.'

Jeannie sat in dumb shock.

'I think you should try and move in with Myra permanently. If you need a hand moving your things I'm sure I could get the roadies to use our van to move them.'

Jeannie turned and looked at Danny. 'Does this mean that I'm not going to see you again?'

'I think that's the best idea, for a while anyway.' Danny said. Once more tears spurted from Jeannie's eyes. She clawed at the door handle and ran from the car.

Danny called after her, but she kept running. He sat and watched her run out of sight around a bend in the road.

'You're some bollocks,' Danny said to himself as he walked into the pub.

Thirty-five

Danny looked down from the choir loft of the church, picking out people he knew by the backs of their heads. The church was packed to capacity with members of the rock fraternity, curious locals, the international and national press and members of the drug squad, all attending Richie's funeral mass for different reasons.

Danny's mind had started to wander once the music had finished. Sean had sung 'I Shall be Released' and now Danny was waiting to sing 'Crazy Dreams' at the end of the mass.

Danny hadn't expected a circus of such magnitude. Earlier, Snake had warned him that the major tabloids from Britain were already in town for the funeral, as well as record company people who had arrived early for the gig.

The Irish daily papers had front-page photographs of the removal and subdued re-runs of the tragic story. The British tabloids veered between 'POLICE HUNT ROGUE PUSHER' and 'ROCK FATHER'S HEARTACHE', showing a picture of Richie's father, staring pathetically at the ground.

Danny stopped listening to the priest as soon as he started his eulogy to Richie. He detested the manner in which priests tried to bring everybody back into the fold, after death.

'Richie,' the priest began, 'found his own way of communicating with God, through his music. That was the language they shared, for doesn't all talent stem from God.'

'Bullshit,' Danny muttered aloud, only to hear a 'Ssshh' of admonishment from Mary, who had come to the loft with him.

Danny threw her a look, which let her know how he felt, and Mary smiled back at him.

There was a shuffle of feet and the sound of people rising. Danny turned to Sean and Frankie. They nodded their readiness, and, as the priest spoke the last few prayers, Danny and Frankie began playing the first few notes of 'Crazy Dreams'.

Danny's voice rang out like a bell through the church while Sean tapped a lonely rhythm on the claves. The two guitars sounded more poignant than a full band. As he sang, tears began to trickle down Danny's cheeks, and his voice caught in his throat. Sean quickly realised what was happening and sang along in unison, covering the tremor in Danny's voice.

The priest came down from the altar and blessed the coffin. The slow procession down the church began.

By the time he had packed his guitar and walked down the stairs from the choir loft, Danny had regained full composure. He took Mary by the elbow and steered her through the door, out into the harsh sunlight.

'Let's go meet the human worms,' Danny whispered from

the side of his mouth as he, Mary, Sean and Frankie joined the throng.

Cameras clicked and people began to push forward to shake hands with the band. Danny's eyes were cold and dispassionate as he listened to the condolences.

* * *

Once the funeral cortège hit the coast road at Clontarf it picked up speed. It sped out the road to Sutton. As they drove, Danny and Sean smoked a huge pipeful of hash.

'Somebody told me there was a wreath from "The Late Late Show",' Danny said.

'I told you, dick-brain,' Sean said.

'Oh, was it you? Anyway, fair fucks to them. It was a nice thing to do in the circumstances.'

'There were quite a few famous people there,' Mary said. 'I saw all kinds of people I only know from television.'

'But sure you've met most of them before,' Danny said.

'I've met them,' Mary said. 'But they wouldn't recognise me in a fit, because the only time I met them was with you.'

'Hold it,' Danny grinned. 'Mary's off on her hobby horse. There'll be another funeral if she gets mad enough.'

Mary scowled. Danny reached across and squeezed her knee affectionately. 'I'm only kidding, babe.'

'It's great weather for a funeral, all the same,' Sean quipped.

Most of the people who had been in the church had driven to the graveyard. They thronged around the grave. Danny watched it all coldly. Richie's brother and sisters stood tearfully along one side of the grave. His father remained stoical as the priest's handful of earth hit the coffin.

'Ashes to ashes, dust to dust.'

A cover was placed over the grave, with fake green grass

tacked to it. The family wreaths were placed on top and then individual people began to step forward to lay their own wreaths and flowers.

'Carry on back to the car with Sean, will you?' Danny said to Mary. 'I'll be with you in a minute.'

Danny detached himself from the crowd, which was starting to drift towards the gates of the graveyard. He walked between graves, reading the names on the small crosses and the gravestones.

He stopped when he saw the headstone he had been looking for. This was Phil Lynott's grave. Danny thought back to the cold January morning when the rock singer had been laid to rest. Tears had tumbled down his cheeks as his hero had been lowered into the clay.

'Hello, Philo,' Danny said. 'I haven't a clue whether you can hear me or not, but you have a pal there now, Richie. Like you, he loved music and he loved playing bass. He admired you a lot and he stood here beside me the day you were buried. If he needs a friend wherever you are and you can help him, do what you can for him, will you?'

Thirty-six

A huge truck took up most of the laneway beside the Baggot Inn. Inside, a twenty-four track recording desk gleamed in the glare of the spotlights. Snake had hired the mobile studio from a company in Wales and now, after hours of running cables to microphones, and more hours of testing all the channels, the engineer was ready to start listening to the sounds of the instruments.

'I'll tell you something,' Snake said. 'This will be the first Irish band ever to break on the strength of a live album. Already four of the independents are interested. On top of that, the majors are all waiting to see what the gig is going to be like. And we know it's going to be fucking great, don't we?'

Neither Danny nor Sean answered.

'How's Owney working out?' Snake asked nervously.

'Great, just great,' Danny answered.

'Does he know all the stuff well?'

'Stop panicking, Snake,' Sean said. 'He'll be all bleedin' right on the night.'

Snake smiled.

'Well, boys,' he said, letting the confidence seep back into his voice, 'it'd better work. This is costing us a fucking fortune.'

'What do you mean, us?' Danny said sharply.

Snake recoiled defensively. 'I'm sorry, Danny, I meant me.'

'Well, let's not forget that,' Danny spat. 'You're taking the chance with the live recording. If we get a deal, you get your costs. If we don't, it's your baby. And Sean is a witness.'

'Look, for fuck's sake, lighten up,' Snake said. 'We're all chasing the same thing y'know.'

'See you later,' Danny said. 'We'd better get this sound check started.'

Inside the Baggot Inn, a small army of people was swarming between the stage, the PA sound booth and the mobile studio. The stage was stacked with amplifiers and instruments. Behind the amps, electrically fired explosive caps were primed and ready, and extra lights had been hired for the night. A huge banner saying 'POISON PIG REMEMBERS' was tacked to the back wall of the stage.

Out front, journalists mixed with curious musicians, who had come to pick up the atmosphere.

'Jaysus, there's more people here at the sound check than we get on a Thursday night,' Sean quipped.

'Let's take a hike for about twenty minutes,' Danny said. 'We'll go to Toner's for a pint – and Sean, stay close to Frankie. Make sure he doesn't start losing his nerve at the big moment.'

'Don't worry about him,' Sean said. 'Frankie'll be fine.'

* * *

'What'll you have?' Sean asked, as they walked through the doors of Toner's pub.

'I'll have a tequila, with the full works, the salt, the lemon, the lot,' Danny said.

'They won't have all the trimmings here,' Sean shrugged.

''Course they will,' Danny said.

'What's with the tequila anyway?'

'It just seems like a tequila night, if you know what I mean.'

'I think you've had a few already.'

'Not a drop,' Danny said. 'But I had a little tokey-poo earlier.'

The tequila appeared on the counter, with a slice of lemon and a small mound of salt on a saucer beside it. Danny took up a pinch of salt and put it on the back of his left hand. He licked the salt. Then he tossed the tequila to the back of his throat and before he could feel the burning sensation, he sucked on the lemon slice.

'That's the business,' Danny laughed, clicking his fingers. 'Another one of those, *s'il vous plait.*'

'Will it be a good gig tonight?' the barman asked.

Danny paused and then cocked his head as he looked at him. 'It will rank as one of the great rock 'n' roll gigs of all time.'

'How's Owney Grace?'

'Compared to what?'

'So you feel that way too,' the barman said. 'How will he be on the gig – apart from wonderful, of course?'

'He'll be out on his own,' Danny hooted. 'Am I right, Sean?'

'Yep,' Sean agreed. 'Out on his own.' The two of them exchanged glances and exploded into laughter.

The door burst open and Snake came in, his movements jerky and speedy.

'There you are,' Snake said. 'Listen, Danny, there's a photographer from *Q* wants to do a picture of you. Fucking *Q*, how about that!'

'I'm on my tequila break,' Danny said impishly.

'Quit larking about,' Snake said. '*Q* is a very hip magazine. They don't take pictures of just anybody.'

'If he wants a shot of me drinking tequila, tell him to come on over. Otherwise, tell him to piss off,' Danny laughed.

'Is he serious?' Snake asked Sean.

'Is he ever serious?' Sean said cryptically.

Snake was flustered. His eyes were darting from side to side.

'Danny, are you coming over?' he snapped.

Danny leaned forward and brought his face very close to Snake's. 'I'm sorry about your deafness,' Danny spat. 'For your benefit I'll say it again. Louder this time. IF HE WANTS A PHOTOGRAPH, TELL HIM TO COME OVER HERE!'

Danny's raised voice caused heads to turn. Snake was

boiling with fury. He bolted from the pub.

'Is there going to be a bit of aggro tonight?' the barman asked.

'You should have been a detective,' Danny laughed. 'Hey, give us another tequila.'

The door burst open and Snake reappeared with a photographer. It was a smart-looking girl, about twenty-five. She had a bright red beret over curls that cascaded down to her shoulders. She wore a black velvet smock over black tights, with small black pumps on her feet.

'This is Evie Cohen from Q,' Snake said, glaring at Danny.

'Hello, Evie,' Danny said, flashing his dazzling smile. 'You're very welcome. Would you fancy a tequila, just to get you in the mood?'

The photographer smiled back warmly at Danny and a glint of devilment flickered in her eyes. 'Don't mind if I do,' she answered.

'So what do you think of Snake then?' Danny asked. 'Is he good photographic material for Q? Did you get a photo of him with his metal briefcase?'

Snake was white with anger.

'Can I see you outside?' he spat.

Danny followed Snake out into the laneway. Snake turned and glared at him.

'I don't know what the fuck you're at, pal, but you're getting drunk now and you'll blow the gig for everybody.'

'Are you concerned about me? Or is it the gig?' Danny snarled sarcastically. 'Are you going to tell me now you're worried about me?'

Snake was flummoxed. He was getting no satisfaction from his exchanges with Danny. He hated to back down, but he knew he would not get the better of Danny, verbally or physically.

'Well, just don't blow it, that's all. There's a lot of money riding on this for all of us.'

Danny winked at Snake and touched the side of his nose with his extended forefinger. 'A lot of money.'

Snake walked the few yards to the street and turned up past the front door of the Baggot. Danny followed. A long line of people curled its way up the lane.

Danny heard a voice call his name. He recognised it instantly. He looked across the street and saw Jeannie standing on the far footpath.

Danny's heart gave a little jump. He felt a sudden tightening in his stomach, Jeannie looked so young and beautiful.

'Hello, Danny,' she said eagerly.

'How'ya doing?' Danny said. 'Are you going to the gig?'

'There's a big crowd,' Jeannie said. 'We don't think we'll make it. There's a lot gone in already.'

"Course you'll make it.' Danny smiled. 'I'll bring you over now and get you fixed up. So, have you moved in with Myra?'

'Only for a few days. I think I'm going to go home for a few months after all.'

'It might be good for you,' Danny said gently.

He led Jeannie and Myra to the side door, where the cables came tumbling through to the mobile studio.

'Louis, these are some friends of mine and they're OK.'

Louis the roadie pushed the door open a little wider to let Jeannie pass. She turned to Danny and squeezed his hand. 'I'll see you,' she whispered.

Danny shook his head slowly, as she was smothered up in the crowd. 'It's all happening tonight, boys.'

Thirty-seven

The dressing-room in the Baggot Inn was packed with well-wishers. Had it been a regular gig, only the band would have been there, but because it was Richie's memorial gig, lots of musician friends had come backstage.

'Hey, Sean,' Danny hissed across the crowded room.

'What's up?' Sean asked.

'The jig is up. That's what's up,' Danny said. 'Would you fancy a lash of this Hawaiian grass?'

'Aloha,' Sean smiled. 'Let's duck upstairs.'

The two friends climbed the flight of stairs to the next landing and leaned against the wall.

'You won't believe this stuff,' Danny said. 'I had so many giggles on it. Will you ever forget the way Snake reacted when I said that shit about the metal briefcase to the photographer?'

The two men laughed heartily, passing the joint from one to the other.

'How's time?' Danny asked.

'We're on in fifteen minutes,' Sean answered.

Snake bustled his way around to the dressing-room. He opened the door and was taken aback by the number of people in the room. He raised his voice.

'Excuse me. Could the band have a few minutes together, just before we go on?'

'Sure, sure,' came the murmured assents, and people began filing out of the dressing-room.

When everyone had left the room except the band, Snake leaned against the door and spoke. 'How's everybody feeling?'

Nobody answered. After what seemed like an eternity, Owney Grace began to babble.

'I ... I ... I feel dead on,' he blurted.

'I'm cool as well,' Danny said, letting bubbles of laughter percolate through his words.

Snake relaxed when he saw Danny smiling. Danny had him terrified tonight. He was like a bomb, primed to explode.

'Anybody like a little Peruvian marching powder to help us on our way?' Snake asked.

'Our rich uncle has arrived with some goodies,' Danny crooned.

Snake reached for his wallet and pulled out a small packet of coke, a razor blade and a plastic straw.

Quickly, all four musicians snorted a line each, sniffling and snuffling quietly.

'OK,' Snake said, 'you've got a minute before you go on. Kill 'em dead.'

He pulled the door open and backed out. Just as he left, he saw Danny, through the remaining chink, starting to mimic him.

'Kill 'em dead,' Danny said, doing a perfect take-off of Snake.

Danny felt his pulse accelerate with the cocaine. His adrenalin started to pump.

'Well, chaps, here we go,' Danny said.

He reached for Sean's hand and gave him a long firm handshake, with both hands. Then he did the same with Frankie.

Owney had his hand out ready. Danny looked at him levelly. He took Owney's hand, and gave him a short one-handed perfunctory shake.

Danny pulled the door open for the others. Sean went first, then Frankie, then Owney, with Danny bringing up the rear.

They paused just outside the door to the bar. Sean gave a nod to Louis the roadie, who signalled up along the line. The taped music died. An expectant buzz went up around the room and then the lights went down. Sean, Frankie and

Owney ran through the crowd onto the stage.

Danny heard Sean hit the drums in a few short bursts. He heard the twang of Frankie's guitar and a deep thud on Owney's bass as he checked his tuning.

A smoke bomb exploded in front of the stage. The throb of Frankie's guitar, loaded with howling feedback, killed all conversation and just as the pitch rose to pain level, Sean played the drum fill into the introduction of 'Designer Aid'.

A roar of approval went through the crowd as they recognised the first few notes. Danny hurled himself around the corner and out through the crowd. He leapt onto the stage, just as the last line of the intro finished. Three flash pans and three smoke bombs exploded simultaneously.

'Hello, Dublin!' Danny shouted in mockery.

Sean played a dead stop on the drums. Frankie finished in time with him. Owney played the next two notes before he realised he was playing on his own.

Snake felt the blood drain from his face. A cold sensation hit the pit of his stomach. The crowd sensed immediately that something odd was happening.

Danny started to speak, slowly and passionately: 'My name is Danny Toner and I'm a living, breathing human. On guitar, this is Frankie Dunn and on drums, Sean Devlin. They are sensitive humans too. We are the remaining original members of Poison Pig.'

A ripple of excitement ran through the crowd.

'Poison Pig began as a stroke. It was born in the sewers of one man's mind and from day one, the whole thing was an act. A lot of you here tonight know that, because you know us. And we really don't have any animosity towards Bono, Geldof, Springsteen and all those people we slagged off. It was just a good scam, an easy way to be controversial and get a name for ourselves, make some dough and maybe wind up in the back of a limo. Sadly, and it's our fault, there are people out there who believed all the bullshit and I have the scars to prove it.'

Danny fingered his nose and delivered the last line with the skill of a wry comedian. The crowd laughed and the laughter was fuel to Danny. He felt totally relaxed. He felt himself speaking slowly and evenly. His brain felt crystal clear.

'The problem is that all of those scars aren't genuine. Some of those scars were bought by money. They were part of the scam. Except I didn't know that guys were being paid to hit me. But credit where credit is due, that was good hype and we all know the value of good public relations.'

'Then Richie died. That was bad for Richie but good for the band. And since Richie died, just a few days ago, one man has pushed to put this gig together for our dead comrade.'

'This man said to us, "If Richie's death can help us, then it's Richie's way of still being in the band".'

Danny started to howl with laughter.

'It's Richie's way of still being in the band.' He mimicked Snake perfectly. 'It's so good, you'd nearly buy it, wouldn't you? You'd nearly like a guy who could come up with one like that, wouldn't you? Except you couldn't like this piece of human shit, this slippery little toad, this coked-out rat of a wheedling bastard. His name is Snake O'Reilly, he's here tonight and I'm going to kill the little fucker.'

Danny pointed down to Snake and jumped from the stage into the crowd, falling as he hit the ground.

Snake paled. He made an instant decision. He turned and ran, pushing people out of his way, his eyes frantic in his head.

Danny picked himself up where he had fallen. Snake had been so scared he hadn't noticed Danny falling.

The crowd began to laugh.

'Come back, you little bastard,' Danny roared, his eyes flashing, as he ran through the crowd.

Snake burst through the crash-door into the lane where the mobile studio was parked. Danny followed him to the door, still bellowing. Some of the crowd followed behind him, in time to catch a glimpse of Snake's heels disappearing around the corner.

Danny was clutching himself with laughter. He walked back through the grinning crowd, a large smile on his face.

The crowd began to chant: 'Pig, Pig, Pig.'

More began to clap along with the rhythm. 'Pig, Pig, Pig.'

Sean and Frankie were grinning from ear to ear. Danny jumped on stage and hugged them both.

At the side of the stage, Owney Grace stood bemusedly, his bass dangling listlessly from his neck.

Danny turned and took the microphone in his hand.

'Poison Pig is dead but we want to play for Richie anyway. If any of you record company people are anxious to get back to your hotels for your expense account drink and women, now's the time to fuck off, 'cos we're going to play some blues.'

A great cheer went up from the crowd. Danny looked across at Owney, who was dying of discomfort. He pulled back from the microphone so the crowd couldn't hear. 'C'mon, Owney. You were such a prick for the last few days. This is your chance to show us what a really nice person you are.'

Owney wasn't sure whether Danny was mocking him or not. He stood undecidedly, until Danny flashed him a smile. Owney jumped back on stage and Danny turned to the band.

'A twelve bar in E.'

Sean counted the four beats and the band pumped to life, pounding out the reassuring rhythm of the blues.

Danny turned upstage, twisting the microphone stand so that he was facing Sean on the drums. Sean looked back at Danny and grinned.

'Hey, Magoo,' Danny shouted over the microphone. 'How're ya fixed for rejoining the smallest Caribbean band in the world?'